ME & MR. CIGAR

ME &
MR.
CIGAR

GIBBY HAYNES

Published in the United States by Soho Teen
an imprint of Soho Press, Inc.
227 W 17th Street
New York, NY 10011

Library of Congress Cataloging-in-Publication Data
Haynes, Gibby, author.
Me and Mr. Cigar / Gibby Haynes.

ISBN 978-1-61695-812-1
eISBN 978-1-61695-813-8

1. Supernatural—Fiction. 2. Dogs—Fiction. 3. Brothers and sisters—Fiction. 4. Adventure and adventurers—Fiction. 5. Hostages—Fiction.
LCC PZ7.1.H3968 Me 2020 I DDC [Fic]—dc23

Interior art by Gibby Haynes
Interior design by Janine Agro, Soho Press, Inc.

Printed in the United States of America

10 9 8 7 6 5 4 3 2 1

For Missy and Satchel

A NOTE FROM THE AUTHOR

As a young child I would lay in bed side by side with my father while he read to me until I fell asleep. Sometimes I was unaware of his departure, while other times I lay half-asleep with the imagery of what I had just heard dancing in my head. The first book he read to me was a picture book called *Pecos Bill*. He read it so many times I memorized it word for word. The second book was *Charlotte's Web*, a savage tale of triumph, desolation and renewal. It was this book that kept a voice in me for all these years saying . . . ya know . . . someday I'm going to write me a book of my own.

I grew up in Dallas, Texas, in the '60s. Part of a classic American family in an idyllic suburban neighborhood. Totally wingin' it in a decade of A-bombs, assassinations and intense social change. I would hope that a young person reading this book would acknowledge the craziness of their own world— to flee from it as well as to embrace it. And above all . . . to reach for the stars.

I have a theory that when a person is born they are given three dogs. The first one shows that you have to live and die.

The second one teaches you how to cope with it. And the third one comforts you. It's a three-dog life and Mr. Cigar is definitely number one.

I tried to tell a story that I might have liked to read when I was a thirteen-year-old. Something slightly dangerous, slightly funny, at that particular age of newfound emotions. Loss and loneliness at the dawn of grown-up love. Oscar has suffered loss and sometimes finds himself both alone in a room and alone in a crowd. It's a wacky world out there. Oscar is in love with it all.

—Gibby Haynes

THE NEXT BEST THING TO GETTING EVEN IS REGRETTING IT

By all accounts, twelve-year-old G. Oscar Lester III was a lucky boy. He lived on top of a hill in the biggest house in town with his father, G. Oscar Lester II, and his mother, Dolores Aims-Lester. The Aims before the Lester was important because, as his mother said, "The Aimses were better than the Lesters and ought to come first." In addition to his mother and father, there were two servants, one butler, a gardener, two cooks and his sister, Rachel Dunbar Lester. Nobody but Mother knew where the "Dunbar" came from, but we all assumed it too was better than Lester.

Rachel tattled on Oscar, was mean to his dog, Mr. Cigar, and even stole Oscar's allowance once and blamed it on the gardener. The gardener was fired, then rehired two days later, when Rachel tearfully admitted the crime at the family dinner table after showing up with a doll worth twice the value of her allowance.

Besides all that, the family was fairly normal for a family that lived on a hill in the biggest house in town with two servants, one butler, a gardener, two cooks and a dog named Mr. Cigar.

From all appearances, life was good for Oscar, and especially today, because it was Saturday. He could wake up late because his mom was at the club, and Big Oscar was playing golf. Oscar had all afternoon to walk around City Lake with Mr. Cigar. Then they would run home through the woods and eat pork and beans and tuna-fish sandwiches, because that's what the cooks made on Saturdays when Dolores Aims and Big Oscar were not at home.

Oh, what a Saturday it was. There wasn't a cloud in the bright blue sky. It was spring. The trees were just now green with blossoms of every kind and color all over.

This would be a great hike. Oscar had a stick in case they found a snake, two hard-boiled eggs in case they got hungry and a compass in case they got lost. But really, they didn't need a compass, because they could see the top of Oscar's house from almost everywhere, except from the woods.

City Lake Park was fun—full of frogs, fish, snakes, raccoons and even opossums, and a rare fox or two. The front side of the lake had picnic tables and cooking pits for all the families who liked that sort of thing. There was a huge field of bumps and trails where all the kids Oscar didn't know would gather and ride their bikes. But the back side of the lake was Oscar's favorite. It was the side of the lake where the wild things were less afraid. It was easier to catch crawdads on the back side. And if you turned over ten rocks, you would either find a snake, a scorpion, or both. Raccoon tracks were everywhere, and one time Sheriff Podus shot a three-foot-long alligator there. Nobody would swim in the lake after that, until they realized the alligator had been stolen from the city zoo by high school kids as a prank.

Beyond the back side of the park, the lake turned into Mountain Creek, which was well named because it wound up running into the No-Name Mountains (that's the name). Sometimes a hungry panther would wander down Mountain Creek to steal a chicken from Gebhart's Chicken Farm.

Oscar's hike today would take them a half mile up Mountain Creek, through a field where wildflowers would rise up every spring and paint an area the size of two football fields with an astonishing array of colors. Alongside the creek, halfway through the field, the ground started getting wet and wildflowers gave way to saw grass announcing the beginning of an impassable plot of land called Opossum Swamp. Only a fool would walk through this swamp. So, to get to "the woods," one would have to walk around this muddy wasteland. It was at this point where the top of Oscar's house would disappear. The possibility of getting lost was greater because the oaks that lived in the woods had enormous, high-reaching limbs that seemed to be woven together from tree to tree. And at this time of the year, the vines and branches were so thick with leaves, it seemed like the entire forest had just swallowed up the sky.

Beyond the wildflowers and swamp, it was a half mile through the neck of the woods, across a one-lane bridge, then a quarter mile to the school bus stop and up the hill to Oscar's house, where pork and beans and tuna-fish sandwiches would be waiting. Oscar always walked briskly or even jogged through the woods because this was an uncertain place where navigation was difficult and attainable only through experience. The oak trees in this forest seemed to have arranged themselves in patterns indecipherable to Oscar. As he walked along, it would suddenly seem like he'd ended up in the same place from where he'd started.

Sometimes there were teenagers in the woods who would come across the bridge from the bus stop. Oscar had seen them before, cursing loudly, smoking grapevine and looking at *Playboy* magazines. They seemed threatening, so he gave them a wide berth, avoiding them at all costs.

It was also in these woods five years ago that Oscar had gotten lost. It was the first time Oscar took the school bus home. When he got off the bus, instead of going up the road and taking a left, he mistakenly went *down* the road and took a left. He crossed over the narrow bridge and quickly became disoriented among the oaks. Oscar wasn't worried at first, but as time went on he had started to become concerned. Everywhere looked the same, and he had no bearings. Then, just as hope seemed to be a thing of the past, Oscar came to a small clearing, and in the middle of the opening was a small black-and-white terrier sitting on its haunches, crying intensely. Suddenly, the dog sprang to its feet and ran to Oscar, acting like they were long-lost friends, wagging its tail, licking Oscar's face and yelping sounds of welcome.

Oscar instantly fell in love with this dog and he even forgot for a moment just how lost he, now they, were. The sun was starting to wane. It would soon become midautumn cold and Oscar had no idea where to go. He knew he had to keep moving and figured he had been going in a straight line, so it would be better to turn back and try to retrace his steps to reach the bridge. The black-and-white dog hung on Oscar's every move. But, as Oscar was about to leave the clearing where he found the dog, the dog stopped abruptly, barked, then slowly started walking in the opposite direction. Since Oscar did not want to lose his companion, he turned and followed the dog. As Oscar began catching up with the dog, the dog started to pick up speed until Oscar was jogging briskly behind his new friend. Then, in what seemed like only a few minutes, right there, only twenty feet in front of the pair was the one-lane bridge—the bridge that would lead them to the bus stop and their way home.

As they crossed over the creaky old expanse of wood and rusting iron, the weary pair cleared the canopy of the forest, and Oscar could see the top of his house outlined in the orange disk of a full autumn moon. They ran past the bus stop, right down the middle of the road, then through the gate and up the hill to the family house. Oscar, more than relieved to be home, walked through the entry and into the dining room, where he had arrived just in time to see the coffee served after dessert. He breathlessly told of getting lost in the woods and being rescued by a black-and-white terrier. His father listened to his story and told him that the family had been worried about Little Oscar, and that he was foolish for getting lost. He then ordered Oscar, "Go to your room. Jenny"—the cook—"will bring your dinner to you there." Oscar turned toward his room, then paused and replied, "Okay, but Daddy, the dog that showed me the way out is on the front porch." He paused again. "Can I keep him?" Big Oscar ended the situation by proclaiming, "Absolutely not! Now go to your room. We are leaving early tomorrow for Uncle Vincent's annual lobster brunch." Without really acknowledging his father, Oscar formed the words, "Yes, sir." He then turned and hurried to his bedroom and closed the door, then opened his window and called, "Here, boy," in the direction of the front porch. Within seconds, the terrier was in Oscar's room and under his sheets, curled up in a ball for a good night's sleep.

Oscar waited until the next day to ask again if he could keep the dog. His dad said no and kept saying no every day for six more days, until he realized the dog had been staying in the house for a week without him noticing. Big Oscar finally gave in, said the dog could stay and asked what his name was. Without hesitating, Oscar replied, "Mr. Cigar."

It had been five years since Oscar met Mr. Cigar, and they've hiked around City Lake many times since. Mr. Cigar had not changed a bit, and Oscar sometimes thought Mr. Cigar could read his mind. Today, as Oscar and Mr. Cigar walked down the hill to City Lake, Oscar remarked to himself that this not only had been a beautiful spring, it was also an important spring. Important because it was the last spring for Oscar before he became a teenager. He wasn't sure if he was ready to be a teenager; he found the older kids threatening at times and he just sort of liked life the way it was. More important, this was his last spring on City Lake because in the fall he would be shipped off to Connelly Boarding School, over five hundred miles away. Oscar was okay with the school because it was a good one and he was an excellent student in any math or science class. Plus, Big Oscar paid for a gymnasium for the school a few years before, so it was okay for Mr. Cigar to live with Oscar in the dormitory.

Oscar's sister, Rachel, was now seventeen. This was an important spring for her as well. She was just finishing her last year at St. Barbara's, the local private school. In the fall she too would leave home. An excellent student and a better-than-average-artist, she would settle for nothing less than Ivy League, and was headed for Brown University. In the past she had preferred the friendship of her private-school friends over the local kids. In the last year of school, however, she had fallen in with some of the troublemakers, like the scary kids in the woods Oscar had seen before. Rachel had a boy-friend, Larry Teeter, who Oscar couldn't stand because he would pretend to kick Mr. Cigar, and he said mean things and sometimes smelled like alcohol and cigarettes.

At the bottom of the hill on this important spring day, Oscar and Mr. Cigar turned into City Lake Park, passed the picnic tables and cooking pits and arrived at the field of bumps where the kids rode their bikes. Oscar only recently found out that Rachel and Larry sometimes went there and that everyone called this place Devil's Ditches.

On the way to the back side of City Lake, Oscar and Mr. Cigar spent the afternoon lifting up rocks, lying in the sun and skipping stones in a particularly calm part of the lake, where the flat pieces of limestone seemed to float on the water's surface forever. Mr. Cigar chased a rabbit that disappeared into a hole, and Oscar found a small garter snake that he held for a few moments before returning the reptile to its rocky lair. As the shadows started getting long, the pair continued up Mountain Creek and across the field of wildflowers, around Opossum Swamp approaching the last leg of their journey— the entrance to the woods where the giant oaks live and the forest swallows up the sky. Mr. Cigar barked and slowly picked up speed as they began their swift passage through the neck of the woods, over the bridge to the bottom of the road, where they would find themselves only moments away from home, pork and beans and tuna-fish sandwiches.

The forest was extra dark today as the sun dipped behind some clouds. But Oscar and Mr. Cigar had made this trip many times before, so navigation was not an issue. Soon, they came to the bridge and gingerly stepped onto its creaking mass of wood. As was his custom, Oscar stopped halfway across to stare at the shallow creek that flowed maybe ten feet below. It was at this point that Oscar realized that they were not alone. Coming from the other end of the bridge, between them and their tuna-fish sandwiches, was Larry Teeter, Rachel's icky boyfriend. He was with three of his cronies that Oscar vaguely recognized, and they were approaching quickly. Oscar considered his options, but there was really nothing the pair could do but hold their ground and hope for the best. The four of them, faster and stronger than any twelve-year-old, were all wearing big, unfriendly smiles. Oscar knew that nothing happy was going to take place on the bridge that day.

In an instant, the four teens had them trapped against the short railing of the bridge. Lurching forward into Oscar's face, Larry Teeter, like a giant menacing baby, said, "Oh, look, it's Rachel's little brother." Larry then began laughing in a distinctly unfunny way. Oscar froze with terror, reeling from Larry's gross breath. Larry Teeter's face was so close to him that Oscar could smell cigarettes and onions and even see dried mustard in the creases of the corners of his lips. Larry grabbed Oscar and lifted him up like he was going to throw him over the bridge. Mr. Cigar growled and lunged with teeth bared. Larry dropped Oscar, turned his leg and kicked Mr. Cigar as hard as he possibly could. He struck Mr. Cigar square across the head and chest, sending Mr. Cigar sideways and spinning over the railing of the narrow bridge, landing wickedly on the embankment by the creek some ten feet below.

Oscar charged Larry with a wild man's scream, and Larry, who was laughing harder now, calmly delivered an uppercut, hitting Oscar right in the solar plexus. In agony, Oscar dropped to the splintery planks of the creaky bridge, violently convulsing and gasping for air. Larry and the others, laughing still louder now, slowly turned and walked back in the direction from which they came. They were heading maybe to the bus stop, maybe to Devil's Ditches, or maybe wherever they wanted to go.

Still unable to breathe, Oscar genuinely thought he was a goner. Somehow, at the edge of pure panic, he managed to exhale, giving his hungry lungs room for a blast of much-needed oxygen. Oscar was relieved for a moment, then he instantly sprang to his feet, ran to the other side of the bridge and saw Mr. Cigar lying on his side motionless just a few feet from the watery edge of Mountain Creek. Adrenaline pumping, Oscar bolted down the embankment screaming at the top of his lungs, "Mr. Cigar! Mr. Cigar!" Practically falling to Mr. Cigar at the edge of the creek, unable to think and all but paralyzed, he stared wide-eyed for a moment in disbelief. Then, softly kneeling to comfort his injured best friend, he began lightly petting him, listening for a breath. Oscar was desperately hoping for a twitch of a paw, the wag of a tail, any sign of life, anything . . . Nothing. Oscar, now thinking with a bit of reason, lifted Mr. Cigar into his arms, scrambled up to the road, then ran toward home as fast as he could.

Hoping against hope, Oscar thought if he could get Mr. Cigar to a hospital soon enough, the dog could be saved. Running and running, he finally reached the gate at the bottom of his driveway and sprinted up the lawn, over the bushes, then breathlessly climbed to the porch. Chest heaving and sweating profusely, he looked up. Suddenly, the front door sprung wide open, revealing his father holding a flashlight, followed by his mother, martini and cigarette in hand. They were definitely in a hurry, both with looks of concern. Oscar's father stood erect, looking surprised. His mother dropped her cigarette and semi-hysterically ran toward Oscar, exclaiming, "Oh my God, Oscar, are you okay? . . . Lawrence told us all about the accident. He's really worried about you. Three of his friends are searching the woods. We were all just leaving to go down there and find you. Is Mr. Cigar all right?"

"No, Mom," Oscar replied. "He's hurt bad and, we gotta get him to the hospital."

"Oh, sweetie. I'm sure he'll be okay," assured his mom. "Your father will take you right now."

Big Oscar pulled the keys from his pocket and motioned toward the car. "Come on, son. We'll be there in ten minutes. Are you okay? What happened to Mr. Cigar?" Without waiting for a response, he said, "He'll be just fine."

Oscar, still tightly holding Mr. Cigar, rolled into the back seat of the family car as they began to back out of the driveway. Looking out the window, Oscar asked his father, "Who is Lawrence? What accident?"

"Why, the Teeter boy," responded Big Oscar. "Larry Teeter, Rachel's boyfriend," he added.

Oscar was dumbfounded. Just then he saw Larry and Rachel walk out onto the front porch. Oscar could clearly see Larry's facial expression. It was the fakest look of concern Oscar had ever seen.

On the way to the hospital, Big Oscar said, "Lawrence was really sorry he surprised you and Mr. Cigar, and when Mr. Cigar lunged at him he said he just reacted from instinct. Son, I know he didn't mean to hurt him." Oscar's father looked over his shoulder toward Oscar and asked, "How did you fall down? Lawrence said you fell down and ran into the woods." Having been temporarily distracted by Larry's ridiculous lies, Oscar returned his thoughts to Mr. Cigar.

"Hurry, Dad! Hurry! I think it's really bad."

The car ride seemed to take forever. The rest of the evening was a blur. Oscar remembered the fluorescent lights in the waiting room, the stern-faced veterinarian, the limp body of his best friend, and worse than anything, the awful words, "I'm sorry, son, Mr. Cigar didn't make it. There was really nothing we could do."

Oscar sobbed all the way home. Blinded with tears, he gently put Mr. Cigar in a small wooden box lined with pine needles and buried his buddy in the backyard at the base of an oak tree. Returning to his house, he was inconsolable. He locked himself in his room and cried late into the night, finally falling asleep a couple of hours before sunrise, dreaming of better times with Mr. Cigar.

Sometime in the early afternoon he was awakened by a knock on the bedroom door. As he opened his eyes, he reached down to pet his dog, and reality came crashing back. Mr. Cigar was gone, nothing could bring him back and that awful Larry Teeter was responsible.

Again there was a knock on the door and Oscar's mother's voice. "Honey, I have some breakfast for you, and there's someone here to see you. Please unlock your door." Still in yesterday's clothes, Oscar reluctantly got out of bed and opened the door for his mother. She had a tray with orange juice, French toast and bacon, Oscar's favorite breakfast. She also had the oddest smile on her face, and as she put down the tray on Oscar's dresser, said, "You must be starved, sweetheart . . . Look who just came to the back door." Oscar couldn't care less, but he looked past his mother to see who had come to visit. At first he saw no one. Then, glancing down, he understood his mother's odd smile. There in the hallway was a small, dirt-covered black-and-white terrier. It was Mr. Cigar. It was a miracle, and it was real! The little dog wagged his stubby tail and limped to the bed, where he and Oscar enjoyed the best French toast and bacon in the entire history of the whole wide world.

How could this have happened? wondered Oscar. How did Mr. Cigar come back to life? How did his heart start beating again, and how did he dig his way out of that dirt-filled hole? But Oscar really didn't care. Mr. Cigar was back—a little worse for the wear, but he was back. Oscar even forgot for a while about Larry Teeter and the incident at the bridge. For the rest of the afternoon, Oscar lay on his bed petting Mr. Cigar, interrupted only by the occasional family member coming to express their mutual astonishment and joy. Everything was back to normal as the sun went down that evening.

Then, around ten o'clock, as Oscar got ready for bed, Mr. Cigar started pacing back and forth on the rug, occasionally pausing to heave his chest and make a funny noise. Oscar wasn't too worried, as he'd seen this behavior before when Mr. Cigar had eaten something rotten from the garbage. Finally, Mr. Cigar stopped, gave one gigantic heave and from his mouth came something strange, very strange. It was unlike anything Oscar had ever seen. It looked like an insect larva of some sort, but it was much bigger than any insect. Not only that, but it had hair and it moved slightly, as if it was alive. Oscar bent over to grab it with a wad of toilet paper, but Mr. Cigar growled and gently picked it up in his mouth and put it under the bed for safekeeping.

Oscar was not especially concerned with Mr. Cigar's actions. Mr. Cigar now had a lot more energy and was wagging his tail happily. Oscar figured the larva puke was something his dog had encountered while digging out of the hole and decided he would clean up the mess before school in the morning.

Oscar hopped into bed with Mr. Cigar and went to sleep and dreamed of the most amazing things—joyous things impossible to describe.

When Oscar woke the next morning, he still couldn't

believe what had happened over the weekend. But Mr. Cigar was still there, alive and well and very much a happy dog. After dressing for school, Oscar looked under the bed to retrieve the thing that had made Mr. Cigar sick, but to his surprise, it was gone.

Where could it be? he thought. Did Mr. Cigar eat it again?

Then, as he grabbed his shoes, he spotted it in his closet. But it wasn't on the floor, as logic would dictate. It was oddly attached to the wall, about a foot off the ground, and it was moving like it was alive. This is weird, Oscar thought, very weird. He was late for the school bus, so he put on his shoes and ran out the door. As he left his room, he looked back at Mr. Cigar, who was guarding the entrance to the closet. Very, *very* weird, he thought.

When Oscar came home from school that day, Mr. Cigar was in the same place as when Oscar had left—lying on the floor blocking the doorway to the closet—and basically that's where he remained for the next two weeks. Mr. Cigar left his post only occasionally to eat or go outside for a brief walk. He still slept at the foot of the bed, but would get up several times in the night and walk to the closet, and quickly return.

Then one Friday, Oscar returned from school and Mr. Cigar was on Oscar's bed instead of his usual place in front of the closet. Curiously, Oscar examined the closet to find the thing missing. Where is it? Oscar thought and sat next to Mr. Cigar on the bed. Mr. Cigar gave him an unfamiliar glance, then rolled over to reveal something remarkable. There, clinging to Mr. Cigar's underside, was an odd, doglike animal that was about five inches long. The little creature stared at Oscar with inviting, humanlike eyes and yawned, revealing a mouthful of tiny razor-sharp teeth. It had fur like a dog, four legs and a tail like a dog. The ears were smaller and pointier than a dog's. Most amazingly, however, this creature had wings—wings that were slightly fur-covered and batlike. Without regard to consequence, Oscar reached to touch the critter, and in an instant, it took flight. After rapidly circling the room several times, it landed on Oscar's desk and then promptly disappeared. What just happened? thought Oscar. What had he seen? Was any of it real? After answering "I don't know" to all these questions, Oscar realized the creature had not disappeared, but had somehow changed the color of its wings to match the color of its surroundings.

Once again the creature took flight and landed near Mr. Cigar, then walked to his belly and assumed the color of Mr. Cigar while clinging tightly to his underside. As the mysterious creature nestled in, Mr. Cigar stretched out in his familiar place at the foot of the bed. Just as Mr. Cigar appeared to be falling asleep, he opened his eyes, looked directly at Oscar's face, winked, and then fell asleep. That's strange, thought Oscar. It felt like Mr. Cigar was telling him something.

As Mr. Cigar slept, Oscar's thoughts raced. What is this thing? Who should I tell? Will they believe me? Oscar heard his sister walk in the front door. Without hesitation, he ran toward the living room screaming, "Rachel, Rachel, Rachel! You won't believe it! You won't believe it! Mr. Cigar has a . . . well, Mr. Cigar made a . . . well. There's a thing in my room that looks like a dog, and it can fly—it can fly and disappear really, really fast. Come see it! Rachel, it's so cool—you gotta see it!"

Oscar abruptly stopped. He saw that Rachel was not alone, but with Larry Teeter. Both of them were laughing and shaking their heads.

"I'm sorry, what did you say?" Rachel asked.

"Mr. Cigar made an invisible flying dog? Mr. Cigar made

it?" Larry scoffed. "When I want an invisible flying dog, I generally have to make it myself or go to the invisible flying dog store. And ya know"—he was laughing even harder now—"they'll charge you an arm and a leg. Even for a slow one." Oscar, realizing how crazy he sounded, turned back toward his bedroom, explaining that he was only kidding and that he was going to do his homework if Rachel needed him for anything.

"Okay?" said Rachel. "You had me worried for a minute . . . That was a pretty good one. You sure you're all right?"

"Yeah," said Oscar, closing his door.

Returning to Mr. Cigar's side, he decided it would probably be best if he kept his new little friend a secret. In fact, best for the whole world if he kept this a secret. And a secret, he resolved, it would have to surely remain.

It was a good thing it was a Friday and that there was no school the next day because Oscar stayed up late that night playing with Mr. Cigar and his new friend. At first, the animal was timid with Oscar, but it soon warmed up to his touch. As the hours rolled by, Oscar was eventually able to hold the little guy and watched in amazement as Blip—the little guy's new name—crawled up Oscar's arm, changing the color of his wings to match the color of Oscar's arm, then his shirt, or whatever Blip happened to touch. And as quickly as Oscar wondered if Blip could do something, Blip would do it. For instance, Oscar wondered whether Blip could fetch like Mr. Cigar, so he threw Mr. Cigar's favorite ball across the room. Before he could say, "Get it, Blip!" the little guy was in the air grabbing the ball and dropping it in Oscar's lap faster than even seemed possible. Think of a command, and Blip would obey. Not only was he smart, but deceptively powerful as well. He could carry Oscar's backpack, full of heavy schoolbooks, effortlessly about the room. At one point, Oscar asked Blip to bring him his baseball bat, and on a whim, he thought, Bite that bat. In an instant, Blip snapped the bat cleanly into two halves.

Mesmerized by Blip's abilities, Oscar continued thinking of things for him to do. Without fail, Blip would honor these mental requests. Over and over, as the night went on, Blip seemed to get faster and more powerful. All the while Mr. Cigar looked on, seemingly nodding in approval. Finally, Oscar lay down, shaking his head in amazement as he drifted off to sleep.

The next day was Saturday, and Oscar looked forward to helping the gardener mow the lawn. This doesn't sound like much fun, but for Oscar, it meant driving the riding lawn mower, which would be even more fun with Mr. Cigar and their magical new friend, Blip, tagging along.

Despite the late night, Oscar woke up bright and early that Saturday morning. The sun was shining, and he was excited to drive the mower and to spend the day with Blip. When Oscar opened his eyes, Mr. Cigar was in his usual spot at the foot of the bed.

Blip, however, was standing on Oscar's chest, wagging his tail and flapping his wings. Blip looked exactly the same as the night before, but he had somehow more than doubled in size, making him now almost half the size of Mr. Cigar. Oscar shook his head in amazement again, now realizing that when it came to Blip, he should be ready for anything.

Oscar dressed, ran to the kitchen to eat breakfast and then went back to his room to get Mr. Cigar and Blip. Blip was now perched on Mr. Cigar's back as he walked down the hallway and to the backyard. Blip's wings were wrapped around himself, and unless you looked really carefully, he wasn't there at all. Once they were outside, Blip sprang from Mr. Cigar's back, flying high above the oaks, which dotted the soon-to-be-mowed backyard. He traveled with incredible speed, did flips in midair and acted just like any other puppy. Except this puppy had camouflaged wings and could fly.

Rachel and none other than lying Larry Teeter walked out the front door.

"Hey," said Oscar limply as they approached him and the wary dog. Larry made a jerking motion like he was about to kick Mr. Cigar. Instantly, Blip dropped from the sky, wrapping his wings around Larry's face and clawing him savagely with rapidly pumping rear legs. Larry, muffled by Blip's powerful grasp, swayed and swung wildly in the air. Oscar watched helplessly and with great wonder as Larry, unable to identify the source of his agony, ran blindly and at full speed across the yard, striking one of the oak trees squarely with his miserable lying face. Bouncing backward, Larry fell to the ground, where he lay motionless. A small trickle of blood dripped from Larry's nose as Blip returned to his perch on Mr. Cigar's back.

Rachel charged down the steps with Oscar's golf club in her raised hand, screaming, "You did this!" Mr. Cigar ran for cover on the opposite side of the lawn mower as Rachel violently swung the club toward him. Blip leapt from Mr. Cigar's back, crossing the path of the swinging club. The nine-iron dropped harmlessly to the ground in front of the lawn mower as Rachel collapsed to her knees, clutching her hand and moaning. The whole scene was then overtaken by an eerie silence. Oscar couldn't understand why Rachel seemed to be in such agony. Blip had only knocked the golf club out of her hand. Maybe she had jammed her finger or sprained her wrist.

Then Oscar got his explanation.

There, lying on the freshly mowed lawn, still holding tightly to the nine-iron golf club and twitching ever so slightly, was the severed hand of Rachel Lester. Blip had bitten Oscar's sister's hand off. In total disbelief, Rachel flew up the steps with one long continuous wail. Missing a hand.

Soon, her scream was joined by all others inside. Oscar mechanically surveyed the carnage surrounding him, numbly acting out of instinct.

While Oscar placed his sister's still-quivering hand in an ice-filled cooler behind the seat of the family's John Deere mower, up walked a stunned Lytle Taylor—son of Dan Taylor, the owner of the landscaping company that serviced the family's two acres of lawn and gardens.

"Wow, man, I saw everything from my daddy's truck. Are you okay, dude? Is that her hand?"

"Yes," Oscar pronounced.

Staring at Larry's unconscious hulk, Lytle said, "Whoa, dude! That guy is totally passed out!"

"Yes," Oscar monotoned.

"Holy crap, dude . . . What was that thing?"

Oscar was in shock. Instead of answering, he turned and ran toward the front door, cooler in hand. Halfway up the steps, his wide-eyed family emerged from the house.

Hoisting the cooler, Oscar nervously explained, "I've got it on ice, Dad."

"Good, son," said Big Oscar.

Within seconds, Mr. Cigar, Oscar, his parents, Rachel and her recently detached hand were all in the family car, speeding to the hospital. Oscar looked back toward the house as they drove away.

Lytle Taylor, still on the front lawn, was staring

upward—Oscar could see Blip outlined against the cloudless sky. His able wings propelled him north toward the No-Name Mountains.

Blip was never to be seen again.

Five years have passed since that most memorable of springs. In those years, many things have changed, both for Oscar and for those affected by the remarkable events leading to the unexplained appearance of Blip and the hideous injury to Rachel Lester.

Sadly, Rachel's hand was unable to be reattached. Despite that issue, she made as full a physical recovery as possible. Psychologically, however, it remains to be seen. At the hospital, Rachel insisted she was attacked by a flying dog-like creature, but the doctors just nodded kindly, explaining to the family that people often say odd things while in a state of shock. Everyone else just assumed she had tripped and fallen with her hand under the lawn mower. Oscar was able to avoid giving any explanation as he was looking toward Larry Teeter and the oak tree when the accident occurred. Unable to attend Brown University as planned, Rachel remained home the following year, undergoing rehabilitation. During this time, she became amazingly proficient with her remaining hand. Her artistic skills flourished, and she was accepted to the Rhode Island School of Design.

Now a highly successful artist living in New York City, Rachel sells her paintings for tens of thousands of dollars and attributes her success to an invisible flying dog. She is famously eccentric for insisting on such, but no one is really bothered by it—especially her art dealer, who makes a tidy dollar selling her paintings to the upper echelon of the art-collecting community.

Larry Teeter, on the other hand, was slightly less fortunate.

Luckily, he experienced no permanent brain damage from his collision with the oak tree, but his relationship with Rachel suffered to the point of being nonexistent. As her recovery progressed, he became increasingly bitter, and soon they drifted apart. Unable to attend college, he worked a series of menial jobs. Contrary to Rachel, he blames all of his problems on an invisible flying dog. Oscar has not seen Larry in years and considers himself a lucky man for that state of affairs. Mr. Cigar, while continuing his mysterious ways, most certainly shares a similar perspective.

In the years subsequent to the dismemberment suffered by Rachel, G. Oscar Lester III—the G stands for Gerald (or "Gerry" as Big Oscar was often called)—has found himself at the crossroads on more than a few occasions. To the casual eye, he's a normal, happy teenager, but the events set in motion by that most unusual of springs have set him apart quite significantly. He had some good help along the way. But strange things happen when strange things happen, and it remains to be seen just how strange these things really are.

THE STORM BEFORE THE CALM

Talking to him? Can't even describe it . . . Definitely a feeling but not an emotion, almost an involuntary reaction, instantaneous, at the speed of thought, in the most efficient manner possible. He is literally my right-hand man; he sleeps when I sleep (I think). And in terms of my needs, he simply does what needs to be done without judgment but at the same time with a certain gentle wisdom so as to add a layer of respect or at least kindness to my assorted nefarious activities.

He can run for five minutes and stop motionless without even breathing hard. He never eats. I can almost see through his eyes, and I swear on several occasions I've observed him communicating with insects. He's white with a blackish head, he weighs twenty pounds and right now he is jogging thirty feet in front of me with five thousand dollars' worth of MDMA in his mouth. He is my dog. His name is Mr. Cigar, and this is the mellow part of our afternoon.

I would say sketchiest—but what is sketchy is the fact that five thousand dollars' worth of MDMA is going to turn itself into twenty thousand overnight. Even sketchier, thousands of kids and a DJ are going to kick in an extra who-knows-what, and all I had to do was make a few phone calls and figure out who to pay to get fifty Porta-Potties and a killer sound system to a ten-acre pasture on the edge of a stunning limestone sinkhole/cave complex locals call Honeycomb Falls. Tonight is easily the biggest of our Why Party events and, with maybe just a taste of guilt, it is easy money. My partners in crime and business, Mr. Cigar and Lytle Taylor (aka the clown), just sit back and watch while our staff basically does everything.

I kind of do the planning and promotion. Our staff and other production expenses are provided for by girl genius Carla Marks and her company, IBC. It's hard to summarize Carla with mere words—other than to say she's like the most important person in my life now and probably the coolest person I've ever met. That's the taste-of-guilt part. Three thousand tickets are presold for this one, and there's nothing left to do but walk a hundred yards out of this ghetto apartment complex, pick up the DJ at the airport and drive out to the event to set the wheels in motion for yet another profitable evening. Basically a bunch of money for doing nothing.

But hey . . . isn't that what owning a business is all about? And: not bad for a couple of high school kids. Right? Guess it helps when you have a magical dog—and the accompanying respect a magical dog most certainly engenders.

SOMETiMES i FEEL LiKE A NUT

As Wikipedia states (and I trust them on this one), "Magicicada is the genus of the thirteen- and seventeen-year periodical cicadas of eastern North America." Curious creatures, to say the least. They live underground for a variable number of years, depending on their particular variety, as large, grub-like worms. Then, for one summer only, they emerge, transforming into an exceptionally loud flying army. The seventeen-year brood is out this summer. They are big and orange and black with red eyes and glistening membranous wings. They are noisy, they look like Darth Maul and the last time they crawled from their underground lair was the summer I was born. Seventeen years without a clue then above ground for one glorious flight-born summer. This is the summer of my seventeenth year, and I swear to the bodies buried in my backyard—there's a cat and a gerbil back there—sometimes I feel kind-of-exactly like a cicada.

Scientists theorize this brood has evolved into thirteen- and seventeen-year varieties because prime-numbered cycles make it more difficult for enemies to predict their arrival. It's early in the summer. I guess it remains to be seen if the cicada strategy is one that I might find personally effective. However, the cicadas are out in record numbers, and their sound is deafening.

WHEAT CHEEPIES

Ahead of me, where Mr. Cigar should turn left toward the parking lot, he suddenly sprints hard right . . . then . . . complete silence. Complete silence, that is, with the exception of the unmistakable sound of a police radio.

I stop dead in my tracks. From around the corner appears a man with a badge on a chain around his neck and a gun on a belt around his waste. Waist. Same thing. He's totally gross in every way. Definitely not the apartment complex security guard. He's a cop, and I'm going to have to dig a grave to explain my way out of this shit.

In almost comical overstated Tex-ass accent: "What are you doing in this housing complex, son? You don't belong here," he drawls, without allowing me to answer. "You know these are state-funded apartments and you are trespassing if you don't actually live here?" Louder and more rapidly, he pesters, "Let's see: You're in the projects to get some dope? You smoke that ketamine? That shit's a trip, huh? Turn around and put your hands against the wall."

Giving me no chance to respond, he spins me around

hard. Pushing me against the wall with one hand between my shoulder blades and the other hand in my pockets, he begins sputtering questions about sharp things and weapons. I shake my head no—and start formulating a believable response to his compromising line of questioning. Spinning me back around, he looks me hard in the eyes and repeats: "So, son, what are you doing in the Shady Oaks Housing Complex?"

Then it comes to me. "My dog . . ." *Gulp.* "My dog, sir . . ."

An uncomfortable pause.

"You talking about that dog that went tearing out of here with something in its mouth right before I rounded this ghetto corner?"

I barely have time to nod yes.

"Now, what do you mean, 'My dog, sir'?" he mocks. "What about your dog?"

I point toward the convenience store on the other side of the parking lot and explain I had pulled in to get a bottle of water and my dog jumped out of the car window and ran into the apartments . . .

"So I parked my car and came looking for him."

Smirking, he nods. "You're in a high-drug-crime zone looking for your dog. Guess you've got all the answers, kid." Suddenly, a burst of static erupts from his walkie-talkie, followed by jargon and cop numbers. He looks menacingly at me. "I've gotta respond to this goddamned domestic situations, son, so if I were you I'd get out of here and never come back. If I catch you in Shady Oaks again, Oscar, you're going straight to jail . . . or worse."

I manage a: "Thank you. I'm sorry, I guess?"

Walking past the officer toward my car, I'm surprised he can't hear my heart pound.

Shuddering, I feel dirty. He smelled like Axe body spray, and I get the feeling he thinks the duck calls he orders over the Internet come from a river in South America—as opposed to a warehouse in Fresno. I mean, Jesus, good help must be hard to get around here. I sneak a quick glance over my shoulder at his badge. Last name is Acox. I marvel at the understatement. Either he is so stupid he didn't realize he called me by my first name without seeing my ID, or . . . or . . . ooh . . . he could be slyly letting me now he knows what I'm up to. Obviously, he knows me. But why would he do that? He really seemed cop-like in the IQ department. The former seems more likely, but still the latter swings a lot of potential weight. I just need to arrive at my car and get to the airport, then all will be good. Not to mention finding Mr. Cigar.

Walking past the last row of apartments on the second-floor walkway, staring right at me, was none other than Larry freaking Teeter.

ECHOES
OF JOHNSON

Funny: I thought I saw him in front of that same apartment the last time I made a pickup here. I was driving out of the parking lot and someone who looked like Larry walked out of the apartment and lit up a cigarette while staring in my direction. I had definitely seen him one other time in the nearby convenience store, thinking he was just in the neighborhood to score drugs—as one of my various business associates had told me they sell to Larry. He's such a sad loser that I just pretended not to see him in the 7-Eleven—but this time he is thirty feet away and staring directly into my eyes.

"Hey, Oscar . . . I haven't talked to you in like forever."

Yet another awkward pause as I'm stopped dead in my tracks once again.

"Oh, wow. Hey, Larry. This is crazy."

"Yep," he says. "Where did Mr. Cigar go? I saw him running off over that way."

"Oh, he'll be here in a second. He probably ran off to take a leak. Or two."

Motioning toward my car, chuckling, I slowly begin to move in its direction.

Larry's phone rings, and without looking at it, he says, "I gotta get this—it's probably my mom. Good to see you, Oscar."

"See you, Larry," I manage. "Good luck, man."

Turning toward my car, I hear a slightly creepy "Good luck to you, Oscar."

It's followed by the hollow sound of a state-funded apartment door closing, then of course by the obligatory Shady Oaks apartments dead bolt. *Thwap*.

Man! The carefree aspect to my afternoon just flew out the window. The sketch got turned up a few notches. Law enforcement, Larry Teeter and MDMA.

Unexpected combo. Maybe I should change my ways . . . Ha!

APEX
PREDATION

Finally at my car, I slide into the front seat.

Briefly giving thanks to the 250-horsepower, B230FT motor that powers my 1984 Volvo station wagon, I reverse out of my parking spot.

Looking straight ahead, I ease the car into neutral and open up the passenger door.

I put the car into first as Mr. Cigar with the MDMA jumps from apparently nowhere into the front seat. The passenger door closes from the forward motion. Looking through my rearview mirror I see Larry in front of his apartment again . . . talking on the phone, watching me as I pull onto the feeder road. Oh well. I hope he saw the BABY ON BOARD sticker on the back window of my turbo brick.

Why the sticker? Because it makes me look more like a mom and less like an MDMA-dealing rave promoter. Why "turbo brick"? Because that's what car guys call cars like mine after they marry bumper sticker moms.

I kind of feel sorry for Larry, what with the head injury and all. No one really deserves something like that, but it was fucking hilarious when he ran straight into that oak tree. I know that's kind of mean, but Larry did kill my dog.

Technically, he killed him . . . for a whole night, anyway. And that's *definitely* mean.

CHAPTER 6

ZING ...
SPLASH

Rush hour is rearing its ugly head, but traffic is fairly accommodating. Soon, I'm exiting to the airport. Easily on time for the scheduled arrival.

As I look for a place to park, Mr. Cigar who apparently has decided to wait in the car lowers the passenger-side window and hangs his head out for a breath of fresh air.

It never ceases to amaze me how he can do this, or how he can lock and unlock the doors—even direct the AC vents onto his crotch. Don't know what I'd do without him.

Tonight, the main attraction is a Norwegian DJ who goes by the name of Mike.

He's a bit of a mystery man. Plays in a variety of disguises. I think. Don't know what his real name is, but I'm not worried about spotting him.

Leaving Cig in the car, I walk solo into the international arrival zone and once again chuckle at the arriving-passenger-spotting technique I have developed.

The DJ will be carrying a green card with the name MR. CHANG written on it. I will stand in a sea of drivers holding cards with the names of arriving passengers crudely drawn upon them, while I wait for the only passenger holding any card at all. Also, coincidentally, probably the only twenty-something Scandinavian gentleman named Mr. Chang on the flight from Oslo, Norway.

iS THERE? A MAN? BEHiND YOUR CURTAiN?

Like magic, appearing from the multitudes, my DJ reveals himself, a record bag on his shoulder and the green MR. CHANG card dutifully held above his head. Extending my hand to greet him, I notice a shock of red hair underneath his Orlando Magic trucker's cap. Odd, I think, the only red-headed Norwegian DJ we've ever hired. The vast majority have blond hair and are named Sven or Anders or something.

"Hello, Mr. Chang," I say in a bad British accent.

He smiles. "You must be Oscar. I'm Mike."

It's kind of weird to admit, given the fact I am highly involved and actually profit from the genre, but I just don't like house music. I mean, I like the party and I like the rhythm of the crowd and everything, but I don't really care who's turning the knobs, and the music all sounds kind of the same. It could be Sven; it could be Anders. But tonight it would be Mike. Who knows? He could be a descendant of Eric the Red.

TOMMY
MOMMY
VOMIT

Without any checked luggage, we head toward the parking lot, and Mike begins: "Oh *may-hun*, that was a long flight."

I have to sort of pause for a moment because the sound of his voice is definitely more North Texas than Northern European. I think the two-syllable "man" is what really tips me off. So I say, "Wow, your voice."

He looks at me funny.

"I mean your voice doesn't sound like it comes from Oslo, Norway."

"No, dude, I'm from Houston. Plus," he adds, "my name *IS* Mike—no one from Norway is named Mike."

We both laugh. But to myself, I think: This guy must think I'm a dumb-ass.

Getting to the Volvo, Mike notices Mr. Cigar, who has shifted to the back seat, and says, "Cool dog."

As I back out of our spot, Mike begins with a classic nudge-nudge-wink-wink-style, "So . . . dude. My set was over at midnight last night, but I didn't get back to the hotel till four in the morning, jumped in the shower and barely made it to the airport. Fucking Oslo Airport has nothing but pickled herring and this really strong liquor that people drink out of wooden thimbles. I didn't get one bit of legitimate sleep on the entire twelve-hour flight. Soooo . . . I don't need to take a bath . . . but I'm starving and I'm probably going to need something"—nod-wink—"to help me stay awake."

I crack a wry smile and give a quick "Cig." Mr. Cigar jumps over the front seat and drops a huge baggie of MDMA into Mike's lap.

"That's what the kids call Molly, Mike. Be careful . . . It's kind of good."

"WOOOW," Mike offers, "*really* cool dog! . . . Uh . . . you know . . . on second thought I could probably hold off on the food for right now. Maybe we can just pull over and get a bottle of water or something."

"No problem," I say, and Mr. Cigar jumps into the back seat, noses open the cooler, jumps back over the front seat and drops a Red Bull on Mike's lap (and one in mine). "Of, if you prefer, a Rock Star product."

We both crack up.

"Awesome! Red Bull is totally cool." Looking at an eagerly wagging Mr. Cigar, Mike queries loudly: "What even is that thing?"

"That's Mr. Cigar."

We laugh again as I pull out on the freeway, and I'm thinking: Bet I'm not such a dumb-ass anymore.

Thirty minutes into the hour-long drive, Mike is clearly enjoying himself. He is constantly changing the channels on the car radio, repeating, "Wow, cool," or, "Cool, wow. I think I'm going to puke"

THE ROAD SCHOLAR

Eventually, I can't take it anymore. Laughing so hard there are tears in my eyes, doing eighty miles an hour up the interstate with Mr. Cigar, a criminal amount of MDMA and a DJ from Houston named Mike. I'm nauseated—no lunch and I'm kind of prone to carsickness. Good thing we're getting close to the gig.

I tell Mike, "I'm not feeling so good. I'm glad I'm not doing any of that Molly. I might not be able to handle it."

"Double wow," Mike says as we ease onto FM 66. "I assumed you saw me dump that huge blast into your Red Bull. I also put a little orange microdot in there. Just to round out the experience."

"Uh . . . What's 'orange microdot,' Mike?"

"Acid, dude. You know: the old Lucy in the Sky with Diamonds. It's super clean . . . I got it off a totally legit Deadhead in Copenhagen."

I feel panicked. "Holy shit, man!"

"Don't worry, dude; it's totally for reals. Homeboy got it

from Petaluma Al in Amsterdam. You'll thank me later . . . The colors are awesome."

Oh, great, I regret to myself, Petaluma Al: the Pablo Escobar of Lysergic Acid Diethylamide . . . LSD.

"No, you don't understand, Mike. I don't do drugs."

He laughs. "That's the same way I am, man. It's a complete misnomer to call psychedelics 'drugs.' I think of 'em as a sort of a mind Band-Aid. When your reality gets scraped, you need a little first aid. I feel so-o-o good . . . Wow, cool, this is great. I'm never going to eat again. Cool. Wow."

I laugh too. Wow. Wow, cool. Mike is kind of funny, though. Actually, *really* funny. Then he lets out this laugh that sounds like Richard Widmark pushing an old lady down a flight of stairs in a funky old noir flick. I'm not sure if I say this out loud or just think it.

"That's what I'm famous for." He cackles and starts up with the wow-cool-wow stuff again.

It's getting kind of crispy at the edges of my field of vision. Why am I laughing?

TEXAS
INSTRUMENTS

The water sheet.

One eight-by-eight piece of framed sheet-like material with embedded tubing removes moisture from the air and can provide enough drinking water for ten or so people on a continuing basis. The system is solar-powered, and the harvested water comes out at just above the freezing point. So not only does it provide drinking water, it provides cooling too. Kind of monumentally bitchin'. The water sheet is the hallmark product of the Itty Bitty Corporation, which has made inventor/founder Carla Marks one of the tech world's most talked about people. No doubt its soon-to-be first trillionaire as well. The prototype had its first public demonstration about a year ago, dropping the jaws of Nobel laureates around the world. The technology behind the water sheet is astonishingly simple and in some respects like jumping over the moon: A simple concept . . . it's just how the fuck are you going to do it?

In a nutshell, the water sheet is two technologies. One new, one old . . . married by a concept called rejection/attraction theory, or RAT.

The result? An insanely high-tech subatomic perforated hyper-polymorphic anti-surface. I shit you not. It feels like a rough-to-the-touch piece of fabric, which is pretty cool because not only is it self-cleaning, its multilayers (trillions of 'em) are constantly remanufacturing themselves—transferring properties to one another at a predictable number of layers above or below itself. By some technical standards it can be argued that it's never really there. Hence the "anti" in the surface name/description. That crazy anti-surface is then covered in/integrated with an (unbelievably) intelligent liquid in which an innumerable number of molecular-sized machines are suspended.

Innumerable in the literal sense: *impossible to quantify*. Its magnitude can't be determined at any particular one-trillionth of a trillionth of a trillionth of a second, because it's fluidly dynamic. Plus, it's only theoretically known as to how many machines are actually possible; it's an almost non-segmented curve. But, just for the heck of it, one time me and Carla computed a static machine number out to a googol—"if only to challenge," as Carla put it, "the absurdity of an unimaginably large number." The model still held water, so to speak.

Ordinarily, one wouldn't know so much about the Carla Marks subatomic innumerable hyper-anti-world. But I've been interning at IBC for about five years, starting a week after my twelfth birthday. That probably had a lot to do with the way me and Carla met.

DESTiNy MANiFEST

One day, as an eleven-year-old, I happened to be in the lobby of my father's office. At the time he was one of the bigger investment bankers in North Texas mostly working in property and oil, not a ton of tech. He was known more as a pure financial wizard, but due to an article in *Texas Monthly*, I guess, he got a reputation as a guy who wasn't afraid of taking chances, especially on new ideas, becoming sort of a bigwig . . . super busy and not around a lot. So, I was in his lobby, on the couch for about an hour one Friday afternoon, waiting for him to finish his "meetings" so we could go the lake house.

Then in walked Carla Marks. She had a techy-looking suitcase. She sat across from me and we just started talking. She briefly described the water sheet concept to me, but it didn't really register at the time. After a while she realized her meeting with my father would not materialize, and that she, in essence, was getting stood up. But she didn't even seem that upset.

Carla pulled out a thermos and a popsicle stick with some

stiff weavy-looking stuff on the top of it. Then she said, "Don't worry, it's all organic," and opened up the thermos. She explained it was hot lemonade and clipped a flat camera battery to the bottom of the stick. Then, with a gloved hand, she held the stick with woven material over the steamy liquid while exclaiming, "Watch this!" There was a sudden burst of steam from the thermos that was somehow contained solely within the material area. Kind of a super-dense, tiny whirling cloud for three or four seconds, then abruptly it stopped. After which Carla unclipped the battery and explained the system was designed to be 100 percent solar-powered, but she had used a battery for "demonstration" purposes. "Plus," she added, "it looks so cool when it's fast like that," and handed me the stick, which now had a large popsicle frozen around the woven material stuff.

"What's this?" I asked.

She responded, "It's lemon sorbet. Well, really ascorbic acid and sugar, but it tastes great."

I wondered if it was one of those health products my dad was using to improve his image. "Is ascorbic acid organic?"

"Sure . . . it's organic chemistry."

I cracked up, and so did she. That was when she introduced herself, when I first learned her name. We've been friends ever since. Carla was the first (and to this day only) adult to treat me like an equal. The popsicle was pretty good too.

LiTTLE DRUMMER BOY

After I finished the "sorbet," she packed up her stuff, having been shined on by my dad, and said, "Goodbye." Maybe she thought we'd never see each other again. But I had captured the whole demonstration on my phone and showed it to my father at the lake that night—and the rest, with the help of a phone call and a few googly-eyed physics professors to validate the process, is history. It blew my father's mind. He publicly beamed with genuine loving admiration, proclaiming that his "son knows genius when he sees it." He was proud. It was awesome. It was cool too because, more than once, Carla has told me she was planning to see some other investor guy from Japan that following Monday. If I hadn't called her at midnight on a Friday night to tell her my dad was completely floored, she could be living in Tokyo instead of Texas, and it might have been a "totally different ball game," after which she always mysteriously laughs.

Being around IBC has been an education. Literally. I was their first and only intern . . . still am. I get to hang out, eat free lunch and learn cool shit. Carla soon became a combination of mother, sister and friend. Almost immediate family. I love immediate families, the really quick ones. She showed me how to weld, how to use her 3-D printers, how to hot-wire a BMW—she owned one and took it as a personal challenge to steal her own car . . . the important stuff.

ALL MOD CONS

She also taught me how to drive her BMW and somehow got me a Texas driver's license when I was fifteen. She handed it to me on my birthday—which is her birthday too—and told me when she was fifteen, her parents became alarmed that she would talk to creatures other than humans, particularly cicadas (the insect). Her parents could attest to her ability to speak to them, but, as Carla puts it, there seemed to be a debate over whether the cicadas were talking back.

"So I was sent to a counselor, as they called it."

I knew it was a shrink. "Wow, Carla," I remember asking, "what did you do?"

"I told him I could speak to cicadas. He pretended he believed me and talked for twenty minutes. Then he walked me out to my mother's car. I opened the car door, turned around and just as Dr. Borthwick said, 'Goodbye, Carla,' a cicada came from out of the sky and landed on my lapel. Dr. Borthwick was incredulous. Looking down at my new friend, I said hello, got in the car and drove away. My mother didn't notice the bug in her car, but later told me I must've had a fruitful conversation with the good doctor, as he'd relayed to her that he'd never met a more normal little girl in his entire life. In observation of my renewed sanity, I decided right then: never to talk to bugs in front of my parents again."

I thought it was a cool story—and the last line rhymed and everything—but the water sheet in Carla's simplest of explanations is part swamp cooler and part cicada wings . . . on highly efficient steroids. I kind of get the swamp-water-cooler part. But not very many people know that cicada wings are hyper-aquaphobic. That means they repel water really well. Additionally, the wing structure is such that it kills bacteria, is self-cleaning and provides cooling for the cicada proper. All that while discharging electrical energy as a by-product.

Who'd've thunk it?

Maybe a girl who talks to bugs.

GRAY GREEN BLUE

I'll never forget the day my father came home from work early and announced to the family, while opening a bottle of champagne, that Carla Marks had indeed subverted the zeroth law of thermodynamics, and temperature, in fact, had more than one dimension.

The next day I rode my bike down to IBC and asked Carla if I could have a job. Most of the company's tech was based on a paper Carla published in grad school. It was largely ignored at the time, but now had created so much demand so quickly that my father maintained a second office at IBC where he spent the majority of his time. He became a lot busier, but due to my internship, we actually got to see each other more often. New things were happening every day there, and it became apparent that my dad was going to be CEO of a crazy-important international concern.

The cost to manufacture the water sheet was only fifty-three dollars per unit, and surprisingly, the R&D, or fixed costs, are super low since most of IBC technology was developed out of Carla's college-era research. The margin is so huge, my dad used to say, "Oscar, you'd better not become a spoiled rich kid," and threatened to "love me to death" if I did.

Soon, governments began knocking on Carla's door. The water sheet and IBC's related technologies prompted ominous questions about the current international political structure. The solar power aspect to Carla's invention, seemingly a sideshow, was poised to affect the type, cost and availability of basic world energy needs in a significant way. People were getting nervous about a potential "farewell to fossil"–type event.

Needless to say, security got tighter at Carla's and IBC. I was kind of the mascot there. Or maybe the "cute kid" who was always hanging around asking questions.

Then, thirty-three days after I turned thirteen, my father died in a car wreck on the Chickasaw Turnpike in southern Oklahoma.

LAKE EMERSON AND PALMER

G. Oscar Lester II had hosted a technical presentation of IBC tech at a government/military facility somewhere in the Arbuckle Mountains. When driving home, he apparently lost control of his car, which rolled down an embankment and burst into flames. He died instantly, they say, and my life changed forever.

My sister, who I guess will always hold her mishap with Blip against me (what with getting her hand bitten off and all), was due to leave for art school and moved to NYC about a month after my dad's funeral. Ever since, I really only see her on major holidays. With a few phone calls a year and visiting her in the city one spring break, our childhood together was basically over. Even though it really ended the day her hand came off, it was definitely final when the rest of her body actually moved away.

Almost a year after my dad's death, my mother officially started dating her dead cousin's husband. I got the distinct feeling, however, the relationship had been unofficial for some time prior. The guy had appeared kind of overly clingy at the funeral. Anyway, they seemed sort of happy together. He was kind of nice, plus he owned two car dealerships and a ton of land with oil and gas wells on it. She was the grieving widow with a convertible Bentley and took private jet flights to an island off the coast of Florida (they called it Sand Castle—not Sand Castle Island, just Sand Castle) where she began to spend most of her time.

KRAKATOA: EAST OF JAVA

I hung in there for a while but finally quit baseball last spring, casting aside one the few remaining vestiges of my childhood. Which pretty much disappeared right after my father's funeral. However, that situation did give me the opportunity to pursue my promoter thing, which, despite it all, has turned out to be kind of a groovy deal.

My school experience has been fairly normal, it seems. I try to go as little as possible. I've never done any homework with the exception of writing papers, yet still I'm going to graduate a year early in the top 10 percent of my class. My sister chose the private-school route, but I went public. It was closer and had better baseball. Ever since my fifteenth birthday, I got out of class at noon and went to IBC under the ruse of some "work release"–type arrangement.

School proper is crazy simple, but I learned a lot at IBC.

Carla, who went to public school as well, says that public schoolteachers are basically helpless because not only are they underpaid, they're forced to dumb it down to make it look good on paper so the school district will get its funding from the state or from whatever corporation happens to be in favor with the current administration.

"State, local and federal," Carla says, "the worst of all worlds," referring to free-market capitalism and the dreaded S word . . . socialism. "Why not the best?" she muses. Carla has an appreciation for both.

Naturally, then, in the name of capitalism and in a really social environment, I began throwing parties in the guesthouse at the bottom of my parents' driveway.

THE BEST LiFE ON EARTH

CHAPTER 17

It was a cool spot, with hidden parking and an old horse barn converted to a huge apartment. From the very beginning I looked at the party thing as primarily a business adventure.

The fact that you meet crazy new friends and have sort of a blast is really just a welcome side effect. It's how I re-met the clown. Which is awesome. Nonetheless it is a business . . . I guess.

The first one's always free, kid.

So for party numero uno there was no cover, free beer, a cheapo sound system with playlists I downloaded from some generic IDM Google Cloud. It lasted till 5 A.M., 250 people came and there were a ton of older kids, which took me by surprise. There was also a broken window and a toilet issue. In other words a huge success, legendary actually (as far as school lore goes), and as planned it proved to be an excellent advert for future such endeavors. The second party I got a real DJ, hired some low-key security and charged for everything. Even used the kitchen for late-night catering.

One party I decided to put weed in the chocolate chip

cookies, graduating to mushroom punch then eventually MDMA. No one knew where it came from because I used an unnamed friend in a clown suit to distribute the "party favors." For a nominal fee, of course. Actually, market price. It seemed like a super-groovy thing. I was making money, people were having fun and most important, no pressure from the authorities . . . no pressure, that is, until the second annual Halloween bash, when cops showed up at 3 A.M. and wanted to talk to the clown. The clown had long changed into his street clothes, and nobody got arrested, but the party got shut down early and I was now on their radar.

TRISTATE TERROR

So I woke up the next afternoon, made myself a crema-laden espresso and decided to go legit . . . sort of. Carla was really the motivating force toward legality . . . sort of. She knows/ knew about the party aspect of the parties but was unaware, as far as I knew/know, about my side business with the clown. She'd actually attended a few of the events, somehow knew of the police involvement the previous evening, and called me (really scolded me). Then she offered her company to sponsor the first legal gig.

THE PLYMOUTH WiN-YOU-OVER BEAT GOES ON

IBC put up the cash for the preproduction; we got an advertising budget, rented a PA, lighting gear, some portable toilets, trailers, etc. We got a couple more guys that looked like security, and bam—we used the ten acres behind the IBC research facility. The party went from twelve noon to sunrise in the middle of July (which was the name we used for the party). Fifteen hundred people showed up at fifty a head.

Carla's water sheets provided water for the crowd and air-conditioning for the tent.

Everybody was cool (literally, again). We all had fun and we walked away with around thirty grand plus profits on the sale of party favors. We did another Why Party a few months later called Halloween Overnight.

We sold two thousand tickets in advance, but another thousand people showed up. Our parking lot was filled and people began parking across the FM in a sort of uptight neighborhood. We paid for cleanup the next day, but apparently the neighborhood had been traumatized by the behavior of some of our partygoers. There had been a naked couple caught "sleeping" on the ninth green of a nearby golf course and a few other amusing/amazing situations.

The local authorities, however, were not amused, and amazingly, we could never use that location again. We made a ton of money and developed a decent team to pull it off. However, me and the clown were both graduating from high school and going off to college soon. I guess. So, despite our "success," we decided to throw in the towel. Throw in the towel, that is, after one final big party. A last hurrah, as it were: a big stage with a big light show and a legitimate world-class DJ or two. In a hassle-free, stunning outdoor party environment.

Typical senior-in-high-school-type shit. Only up a few notches.

THE BRIDGE OVER THE ROOT CANAL

We have prepared for around four or five thousand, but who knows how many will walk up expecting to buy tickets at the site. Honeycomb Falls is on private land about fifteen miles south of IBC headquarters. It's an amazing spot with a maze of Spanish moss and waterfalls that have turned the limestone into a giant spring-fed Swiss cheese ceiling of water and sunlight. Pretty cool, and much of the park will be lit with a new IBC "mystery system," which Carla tells me is tiny smart video cameras/a monitor system that can be deployed en masse, to the billions, via a film of aerosol "smart gel."

It's the same concept as the water sheet but in a different suspension. I say "mystery system" because very few people have seen it in action or even heard about it. As far as the public is concerned, Carla Marks's only invention is the water sheet. Which makes tonight's light show extra cool.

GARY THE BEAVER AND HiS FRiENDLY DAM

Both Carla and my dad's replacement, Jack Ogilvie, will be at the show tonight.

Jack came to IBC several months before my father's death. He'd been a friend of my dad's from the navy and only recently embarked on a civilian career. I still hang out in the lab most every day, but technically my position is Jack Ogilvie's assistant. Nowadays I hardly ever see him. I eat lunch with Carla at IBC. She wants to know everything I'm up to and gives me tips on stuff I don't really think about, like college, careers, girlfriends, etc. . . . Maybe I need it. With my sister in NY and my mom hardly ever there, everybody's gone from my parents' house.

In ninth grade I began to hang out more and more at Carla's, anyway, often spending the night there, as it was closer to school. I now have my own room in her guesthouse. I can basically come and go as I please. It's sweet. She has a huge compound where Mr. Cigar chases rabbits around in circles. He can somehow corner a rabbit and run it around in a circle for like fifteen or twenty times before the rabbit has to lie down exhausted. Then Cigar gets close to it and barks.

Plus, I'm privy to the details of the craziest tech leaps in recent history, things that Joe Blow won't even hear about for the next two or three years.

THE GiRL WiTH THE DRUG- SELLiNG EYES

Tonight the Itty Bitty Corporation is sponsoring an insane dance party with drug-selling clowns, as they have several times in the past. Which might actually sound insane but to our common credit *we* are patriotically supporting our country and our country is letting the kids do what the kids do. Sometimes the kids do "Insane Clown." Sometimes our country does "Insane Clown." Tonight, I suspect, it will be a little bit of both because IBC will be demonstrating a new technology during the gig. No matter what, that feels multi-level creepy—actually, Big Brother-style creepy, but who's to know? It's only a video system. Or we might all get eyeball cancer when we turn sixty.

I know Carla trusts me. She lets me stay at her awesome guesthouse without even asking.

And I trust Carla. I figure it's the least I/we can do.

We'll let them do mind control experiments on innocent children, and they'll let us have an insane dance party with drug-selling clowns. So I don't really mind a few government contractor types having a good time while checking out a new technology . . . I guess. I haven't seen the aerosol screen application yet. Tonight is its debut. But at the lab I saw a three-dimensional object wrapped in the video screen stuff and it blew me away. It was basically a foot-long object that one second looked like an egg-shaped video monitor, then the next second it totally disappeared.

When Carla giddily showed it to me, she said, "Yep."

My jaw dropped. It made me lose my balance . . . super weird. Spherical pixels and tiny video cameras make it all possible. Up until I saw the disappearing egg-screen demonstration, I thought she had simply (or not) invented a super-cool new video monitor, but Carla's demonstration made it clear it was much more than that. The perfect camouflage, perhaps. It just depended on what the aerosol smart gel looked like at its unveiling tonight. Carla said that whatever the application, it would be impossible to believe, and given her track record I just gotta believe.

When I asked her if it were possible a person could be turned into a walking video screen, she smiled and said, "Uh-huh. And it even works on hair, sweetheart."

AND BEAMS MADE OF BROWN HiT THE GROUND

Pulling off at the farm market a quarter mile from the party . . . it hits me like a brun of ticks. The closer we get to everything, the farther away "nothing" becomes. The weird lightness in my stomach is intensifying. In fact, everything seems to be intensifying. Without knowledge of how we got here, I watch myself park in the event-staff lot next to the office trailer. The clown is there, happily waiting for the party favors. All of a sudden I'm throwing up in the Porta-Potty.

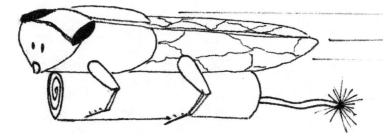

When I opened the door, there were a ton of people milling around, the sun was going down and as my face felt the awesome embrace of that cool evening air I instantly went from feeling dizzy, sweaty and sick to being absolutely sure I was solidly in love with the world and the world in turn was solidly in love with me. As sunlight gave way to light show, my responsibilities gave way to *what the fuck?* The few things I'm supposed to do, at this point in the evening, become randomly unclear then completely unimportant as my field of vision fills with vibrating night glow. Nondescripts.

An overwhelming desire to be with my people while completely without knowledge of what or who my people might be. So off into the hoo-doo night I go, undaunted and afraid . . . everything all at once . . . lights cracking colors . . . humming loudly while hundreds of people glide around me in total silence, only occasionally to be heard whispering, in the distance, unimportant things of grave concern. It takes me a while before I realize that the reason everything is silent is because everything was loud. I drift away from what later I will identify as music and find myself exploring the limestone formations that line the walls of the sinkhole at Honeycomb Falls. The sinkhole itself is at least seventy yards wide, with about half of it collapsed to form a gigantic beach with 180 degrees of waterfalls, behind which are caves of dripping moss and roundish window-shaped rock formations, some of the holes deep enough to step through. Apache Indians used to camp here and around the nearby spring-fed creeks. Then the white settlers moved in and called it Honeycomb Falls, later to find out that the Indians called it the Apache word for "honeycomb." Well, that's the local legend, anyway, but I bet they were really Comanche Indians and I bet they called it whatever the Comanche word for "super-trippy place to hang out" is. Because it is super trippy, and there is always something new to think about . . . always . . .

Behind the falls, feeling the lights . . . The party glistens through the filter of a hundred yards and a wall of rushing water. For a while . . . I don't even know how long. Maybe an hour. Maybe a thousand years. Leaning forward through the cool liquid sheet, face accidentally making contact with reality, I notice the view to be a slightly more focused affair than before. What earlier appeared to be a close-up of a slice of toast has now revealed itself to be a stage and a crowd of people, hundreds and hundreds of dancing people in a large, grassy field with three or four humongous oak trees. Not your run-of-the-mill oak trees but *Roger Rabbit*–style oak trees . . . giant ones . . . glow-in-the-dark, beyond-belief oak trees. Disorienting. Oddly animated. Well beyond real. Carla Marks has done it again. They are trees, I'll give 'em that . . . beautiful old oak trees, but made of light, or high-high-high-definition video . . . photo resolution four-dimensional cartoons.

Pasted onto themselves. Dis-fucking-orienting. So with mind blown, muddy shoes and a stick in hand named Yard Boss, entering the pulsing crowd was nothing less than an exercise in mass hypnotic freedom. At the edge of the crowd, an old man with long gray hair approaches me. Touching my shoulder, he looks me square in the eyes and says, "Mau-Mau the flak catchers." Stumbling past, I look back and he is nowhere. Maybe even no one. Possibly nothing at all.

The confusing rumble of silence has now become music and the most amazing rhythmic experience ever. A large oak in front of me turns into a giant dragon head then totally disappears. I realize now, house music is totally cool—I hadn't given it a fair shake. The tree now reappears as a weird box of cookies . . . I think. A variety of off-scale primates dancing nearby reveal themselves only at the edge of my vision, and their presence is comforting if not directly verifiable. I feel at ease with my furry friends . . . collectively bouncing up and down to this unheard music. Multiplying and dividing at will. What began as voluntary movements have now become an effortless flow as trees turn to insects and back into clouds. I feel good. Yes, I've finally found my people. Not that it's super heavy or anything. But my people turned out to be this jovial array of misshapen primates playfully dancing upright in a void of myopic singularity. No big deal.

THERE'S A RED HORSE OVER YONDER

It seems like minutes to the hour, or it could be hours to the minute. I can't really judge time as what I'm experiencing isn't what I'm experiencing. It's only a description of the experience, and that gets tricky. The devil's in the details with reality, and when description is the only option things can get left out or added in a dozen different ways. You gotta be quick. Stay on top of it and goooo with the flow.

So with the flow I go, finding myself in front of the stage.

My primates are with me, and the DJ has a square-shaped campfire for a head. The music is so much more than sound. At least it's being described that way.

It's so weird—if I think about breathing I have to think to breathe, and it's totally confusing because sometimes I catch myself holding my breath, and I don't know if it's because I forgot to not think about breathing or vice versa. Like I can't believe what I'm seeing, and I can't believe what I believe, so it totally makes me believe what I'm seeing is real because I can't believe it is—it has to be unbelievable or it isn't real, and thank God it's in slow motion.

Despite the fact that most of my thoughts literally disappear while being irretrievably stacked at a secret location in an unknown portion of my brain, I feel compelled to examine all thoughts before they become unthinkable. Then store them in a place where I at least have a chance to validate their potential believability before they are eliminated from any meaningful historical reference. Jesus, thinking about thinking is hard work, but I can't stand the idea of losing even useless information in the thought-sorting process. After all, life is too short to waste time on anything that's not (unbelievably) real. And not only that; how long have I been here? How long will this last, and—oh no . . . time . . . then, oh yeah, time is beginning to mean something. At some point this has to end. The bears are starting to give way to humans, and then . . .

RETURN OF
THE DOG

The music stops. The sky breaks, the crowd sizzles and the primates draw themselves gone. It's only been like seventeen years. Even though I've stopped dancing, as it were, the dancing motion continues from within. I find myself in a crowd of humans. The lights go still, becoming white. I stop for a moment to admire the oak trees, which are now icy bright from trunk to tip. A phosphorescent capillary system waving and weaving itself up to the sky.

I say, "Wow," kind of loud.

A stranger says, "No shit," kind of loud back.

This trip is awesome . . . I can never ever do it again. Even if I want to. It feels like my entire being is covered by a giant sock. I unconsciously follow the crowd toward the parking lot. Oh yeah, I remember . . . I work here. I've got to go to the office, settle up with the clown, generally take care of business and . . .

Where is Mr. Cigar?

Turning in a mild panic, I mouth the word *Cig* and hear a quiet bark from behind.

"Oh, there you are, buddy. I totally forgot about you, man. I'm sorry."

Another bark, a wag of the tail and off we head toward the trailers and my end-of-party responsibilities.

NARCANE

I'd taken however much around five-thirty to six. It's now like three in the morning, my phone is dead and the lights around the corners of my eyes have given way to almost-normal vision. However, the mind effects are still enough for me to be the happiest guy in the hemisphere. I wonder how I'm going to react to the good old-fashioned fluorescent lights.

As we approach the trailer, Lytle swings out of the door, wild-eyed, with a crazed look on his face. That's fairly normal, but he catches my eye and shouts: "Dude! Where have you been, man?"

Oh no. Definitely something's up.

"We got ripped off, man! We got ripped off! That fucking pig was watching me and just—"

"What? Whoa, slow down. We got ripped off? By a pig? You mean a cop? What are you talking about?"

"You won't believe it, man, but he was watching me, and right as I collected from everybody, this guy walks up, flashes a badge and says: 'What's going on? What you got in that backpack, boss? Besides balloons and shit.' I was totally freaked out, and he dragged me into the wheelchair-access Porta-Potty. I don't know why I remember that. We were right over—"

"What happened, dude?!"

"So he was like, What do you got there? What are you selling? That Molly? And starts going through my shit. He's got me handcuffed to the wheelchair rail then starts pulling out twenties while he's going, 'Whoa there, son. You're a dealer. You know dealers go to jail in this county, son. They go to prison with the big guys'—you know, MS-13, Southerns, Texas Syndicate . . . all that shit. He keeps going on about what's going to happen to me, and it's really freaking me out."

Lytle pauses, suddenly worried-looking.

"Yeah, yeah?" I press.

"Then, out of my backpack comes a baggie with about twenty hits in it and he says, 'Looks like at least a hundred hits of MDMA in here,' and shit like, 'Wow, what a shame—that's like twenty years in prison, son. With your other two charges, that's three strikes and you're out.' Oscar! He fucking knew about me getting busted for weed last year in January twice in three weeks. Total freak busts."

"Why didn't you tell me, man? Like I'm going to take away your allowance or something?"

"It's not that, man. I don't know why I didn't tell you . . . but you were in Florida with Carla. It was no big deal, like I said. One case got reduced to paraphernalia, and I thought the other charge got totally blown off—"

"I don't care about that crap, man," I interrupt, but gently, trying to focus. "What happened tonight? Why are you here and not in jail?"

The clown shrugs, incredulous. "Then the cop writes me out a ticket for running a red light. Then he takes the backpack with all our money from ticket sales and everything and says, 'You oughta take care of that traffic violation as soon as possible, son. You wouldn't want your past to come back and haunt you.' Like a total asshole." Lytle looks up. "He just ripped us off. That was all our dough from the gig. Everything. Like forty grand."

Wow. Again, not sure if I say it or think it.

"Yeah, he knew everything, man . . . It was a total setup. I mean, what are we going to do about this asshole, call a hit man? Call other cops? Like, legit cops? Tell Carla?"

Oh, dude.

"Yeah, man," Lytle says.

Fuck fuck fuckity fuck.

"Yep."

Damn.

"Yep."

"What county was he?"

Lytle pulls out his traffic/trafficking ticket. "Here it is. Sergeant Cletus Acox . . ."

Blah-de-blah. Is that name even real?

Lytle's voice fades in a spiderweb blast of neural connectivity. Holy shit, Lytle. That was the same shit-bag cop who knew my name right before I ran into Larry Teeter. (Who wished me luck.) Then thinking out loud. "The cop must have fucking known what I was up to *because* of Larry Teeter, who must have conspired to—"

Somehow the two seem connected.

"Oscar! Snap out of it."

"Huh?"

"Anyway, I was handcuffed to the wheelchair handrail! And Cleet-ass comes back after about three seconds and says, 'Oops. Forgot my handcuffs. See you *never* . . . you should hope.' He definitely got that right. I do hope I never see that asshole again."

I nod, my mind racing. "Yeah, man, same here. Fucking unbelievable. You got busted near the toilets around the corner there?"

"Yep. I was going to find you. Where were you all night, man? I saw you near the front of the stage for a while . . . You were, like, dancing with a stick in your hand."

"You mean Yard Boss?

Lytle flashes a quick grin. "So the stick has a name? Kind of weird . . . but cool, I guess."

"Lytle, did anybody see the police involvement going on? Like people from the office?"

"No, I don't think so. He had me in the toilet pretty quick . . . He was wearing kind of normal guy clothes. Creepy normal guy clothes."

I am trying to make sense of all this, but I know that I'm due inside the trailer. "Speaking of office people, what's going on in the office?"

"Carla's in there now, man. She's waiting for Jack Ogilvie and that company-government dude or something. I don't know. I just want to get out of here. I'm going home. I'll call you tomorrow. We gotta figure this shit out."

"What a drag. I don't know what to say . . ."

Lytle disappears. Cigar is right in front of me again, wagging his tail.

NOSTRALIAN HOLIDAY

Cigar and I walk up the steps into the trailer. The flimsy door swings shut behind us. Carla is leaning against a table—one of those long brown folding lunchroom tables—fiddling with a piece of electronics and an aerosol can.

"Hi, Carla. What's going on?"

If she suspects I'm not in my right mind, she doesn't show it—doesn't even look up.

"Oh, hi, Oscar," she says, peering at the can. "The show was so much fun. I had earplugs in, but it sounded great. I missed you onstage. What were you up to?"

"Uh . . . I was hanging out near the stage for a while. I was in front a lot with friends." My focus is returning slowly. At least the precognition-thought-sorting process is down to a minimum. I think.

Carla smiles, still not looking up. "Cool. How 'bout the light show? I was pleased. It worked a little better than I hoped."

In the silence I nod. "It was awesome, Carla. Like nothing . . . I've ever seen . . ."

"Thanks, sweetie. I think the government contractors were happy too. They should be by any minute with Dan. I'm going to give them a little one-on-one demonstration of the new system then get out of here. I've got an early day for the next twenty years. Oh, speaking of demonstrations, check this out." She finally looks at me. Grabbing the aerosol can, she nods at Mr. Cigar. "Put him on the table here . . . He won't feel anything. You're not going to believe this."

"O-o-okay." My lips feel dry. I obey without thinking. As does Mr. Cigar.

Once my dog is on the table, she sprays a small amount of clear mist toward his back. "It takes about three seconds for replication . . ." Now she picks up the palm-sized electronic device—some sort of controller. It's got two knobs. The one on the left has three settings: Random, Recognize, and Another One. She clicks to Recognize.

"Right now it knows he's a dog, or at least shaped like one. This one is for variations, so . . ."

She turns the other knob.

TRANSITION 22

After a single bright-all-over-his-body flash of light, Mr. Cigar starts changing into different dogs. Like hyper-realistic dogs. A Chihuahua, a Yorkie, a freakin' Portuguese Water Dog.

"Holy shit, that's unbelievable—"

"Believe it, sweetie!" Carla is laughing, switching from dog to dog . . . some hyper-realistic, some comical. The pit bull looked real as it was close to Cigar's shape, but the pug was hilarious because it sort of looked like a pug but with a crazy stretched-out nose.

"Oh my God, Carla."

"This is cracking me up . . . The system is really optimized for the human shape, but this dog thing is crazy. Can't wait to try it on a horse. Wonder if I could make a horse look like a dog."

I start laughing. I feel out of control. Slobbering. I fight to get a grip.

"Like I said, optimized for humans, so variations on the human face are insanely realistic," she says.

She flips to RANDOM. Cigar turns bright white as pink

polka dots travel slowly around his body. All the way to the left, white light all the way to right . . . crazy. On the far right it randomizes every time it goes past the four-o'clock position . . . Mr. Cigar's entire body changes to black-and-white TV static for a second, then . . . crazy twisting photos, people's heads, cartoons and what look to be pages from the Bible. It is so totally real and present and stunning that I can't help but laugh out loud again.

"That was the setting they were using on the oak tree next to me and the furry primates!" I shout.

Carla looks curiously at me. "What?"

"Nothing. It's just kind of overwhelming."

"Ha! Then watch this." She adjusts the program knob to the right.

Mr. Cigar totally disappears. I mean like crazy disappears.

THE FUTURE iS PLASTiC

CHAPTER

29

Wow!!!

My feet move forward toward the cheap fold-out table. Then my hands reach out to touch Mr. Cigar. He's there, all right . . . You CAN see a momentary video-like aberration when I disturb his coat. Fucking amazing, though . . . almost perfect.

"It's kind of creepy, right?" Carla murmurs, as if reading my mind. "Nobody knows about it but you, me, Dan and the government man . . . sounds like a song, doesn't it? Ha ha. No, seriously, the public will know fairly soon concerning the basics of the technology but it will take a while before Joe Blow finds out about the camo thing. I mean, the public has to know and have access. I'm sure there are many applications for the system that even the inventor hasn't thought of . . ." She trails off, staring into the big nothing, then after maybe four beats abruptly returns to the moment.

"What do you mean?" I ask.

"Check it out, Oscar," she says in an almost sexy tone, obviously proud. She hands me the remote control. "Now: How does this work?" I ask.

"Simple," Carla replies, "Two knobs . . . three settings on the left, one . . ." click, click, click "and its continuously variable on the right knob. That one gets more random as you rotate it in the clockwise direction, and you've used spray paint—in fact, there's probably police surveillance footage of you using spray paint, sweetheart—anyway, it's that simple. Just a half-second blast does an entire human body. You spray it on something from four to six inches away, then bam. You're ready to go. Cool, huh? It's effective for about eight hours then turns to dust the size of human skin cells."

It's nuts. I'm holding a *Star Trek*–looking wireless controller, staring at an empty table, but knowing my dog is actually there.

"Oh yeah," Carla continues, "Oscar . . . to make Mr. Cigar visible again? Press that button in the middle; it toggles the video net on and off."

I turn Cigar back on. A smile comes over my face, and I start toggling: off again then on again then rapidly on off on off . . . We both laugh a really good laugh, and I bet Cigar is wagging his tail.

"Now try to get him to lick your hand." I reach toward where I think Cigar is and a partial pink dog tongue comes out of nowhere, folding itself against my hand.

Again, big laughter.

"We don't do tongues at the Itty Bitty Corporation, but we're working on it," Carla says.

"Ha ha ha. We actually are working on it. The teeth are almost there, but to really sell somebody else's face, for the time being, you got to keep your tongue in your mouth and your mouth shut."

I smirk at her. "Nice, Carla."

She hands me the spray can. "Give it a blast, Oscar. Just

a little squirt against the wall . . . It's an interesting effect. First you hold that center button in for three seconds to deactivate Mr. Cigar's net and create a new one. Only one net at a time with this controller. Once a net is deactivated, you must reapply the aerosol. Or you are free to create a completely new net."

"Got it."

With spray can in one hand and remote in the other, I step toward the wall, giddy with amazement, none of it drug-induced . . . well, maybe some.

iF i DiE, FiND OUT WHY . . . EXiT THE TiGER

Before I spray—

The office door swings open. Cigar is still invisible. In walks Jack Ogilvie. Always tall and stately and suited, accompanied by a sharp-featured man in a darker suit and shades. (At whatever o'clock in the morning?) He has a huge scar/deformity on his left nostril. Changing gazes like a robot. No doubt the government/military contractor. Or at least the cartoon version.

"Hey, Carla, I suppose you saw us onstage tonight," Jack says. "This is Colonel Pete Sanders . . ." He nods at nostril-scar dude.

I'm thinking, Wow. A real Colonel Sanders . . . can't be. I've seen the Kentucky Fried Chicken commercials. Is this guy original recipe . . . ? No, gotta be extra crispy.

"Nice to meet you, Colonel Sanders!" Carla offers.

Invisible Cigar lets out a little growl. I don't think anyone notices but me.

"I think I can speak for Pete here . . ." Jack continues. "We were both thoroughly impressed with the new technology,

Carla. The aerosol application is stunning." He turns to me, stiff and formal, his smile as usual: all teeth and no light behind the eyes. "Hello, Oscar. I've known Pete for going on twenty years now. He was a friend of your dad's. We all went through basic together. Colonel San— Oh, Excuse, me. Pete. This is Gerry's son, Oscar. He's been working with me for over a year now."

"It's been a solid four years."

"Okay, Oscar," chuckles Jack. "I guess it has been four years . . ."

"Good to meet you, sir." I extend a hand, finding it difficult to look directly into Nostril Man's eyes. All I can see is his totally psychedelic left nose hole.

"Well, *Colonel Sanders*," Carla interjects, "if you would like to see the camo mode close-up you've actually come at an opportune moment. I'm leaning a little more in the original recipe direction."

I laugh. We two laugh. The colonel and Jack grimace.

Carla says, "Oscar, turn Mr. Cigar on."

Cigar barks, this time more nervously. His net has not been deactivated. I click the outer button once, and out of the virtual ether, a tense and agitated dog—my dog—magically reappears. Ears back. Tail not wagging. Standing on the folding table beside us.

"Voilà," says Carla.

"Ah ha," says Jack.

ENTER THE DRAGON

CHAPTER 31

"Oh my God," says Nostril Man.

Mr. Cigar, highly agitated, growls, locking eyes with him.

The colonel, saucer eyed, lunges at Mr. Cigar, blurting out "Goddamn it, that's government military property, Ogilvie . . ."

Cigar springs forward in return. I've never seen him so aggressive. He makes contact with all four legs squarely in the center of Colonel Sanders's chest—who is knocked back a good four feet. Mr. Cigar dashes out the door and into the predawn night.

"Goddamn it, Jack . . . That thing's immortal?" Nostril Man is sputtering.

Jack is stunned while Colonel Sanders whirls to face me.

"Is that your dog, son?"

Before I can respond, he comes at me, crazy-eyed, arms outstretched. I fake left and go right, stretching past Colonel Sanders, through the doorway, into the darkness after Mr. Cigar . . . with a last glimpse of Carla and Jack—silent faces slack with shock—I sprint behind a row of junipers, pursued by a mysteriously angry Colonel Pete Sanders. But he can't keep up. Making a hard left through a cedar thicket, I lose Nostril Man and make record time to the beach and a hiding spot . . . Before I can even call out for Mr. Cigar, he appears instantly. We both run through shallow water, jumping behind the falls and into a room of sculpted limestone. Totally hidden and alone—lungs heaving, still clutching the remote and spray can—I peer through the cascading water to see if Colonel Sanders is still in pursuit.

A voice from behind asks: "Why so out of breath, dude?"

THIS IS CHINA CLIPPER

I whirl 180 degrees . . . to find Mike the DJ sitting cross-legged with a huge smile across his face. He's holding up a clear plastic container of water. He crinkles the plastic a bit. "Want a drag, man? Looks like you could use it."

My legs feel like jelly. "Holy shit, man, you scared the fuck out of me."

"There is literally no fuck left in my body," he replies.

I pant like Cigar would pant at noon on a summer day, hunched over, staring at him. "Jesus. What are you doing here?"

"Just chillin'."

I grab the water and take three or four chugs.

"Whoa, man, there's like half a gram in there . . ."

"Half a gram of Molly?!"

"Yep."

"In this bottle?!"

His eyes narrow. "Well, significantly less now . . ."

"Ohhh noo!"

"Why?" He's amused and puzzled. "What's the deal?"

"I don't do MDMA."

"That's weird, because I swear your dog dropped like a baggie full of it in my lap when we were coming here from the airport—"

"That's different, man," I say, panting again. "I just sell it, I don't do it."

"That's weirder 'cause I swear you did a major blast in the car right before we got here."

"Again, that's totally different because I didn't know I did it—"

"That doesn't make any sense to me, but whatever . . . I guess you do it now. Jesus, man, I gotta get out of here."

Nice to see you, Mike.

A DATE AT THE MOVIES

We dash out of the cave behind the falls, back to the beach, determined to get to the car and home before the twisted specter of psychedelics rears its brightly colored head once again.

Through the cedar tree and behind the junipers we make our way back toward the office then stop dead in our tracks fifty yards from my parking spot. We're fairly stealthy, but the blacked-out late-model Ford parked next to my car isn't . . . especially since Nostril Man is leaning on the hood smoking a cigarette talking on his phone. His head is on a swivel. What the fuck?

I would call the clown to come pick us up, but my phone is dead, plus Colonel Sanders has a clear view of everything in the parking lot, and with only about a dozen cars left, there is really no hope of evading notice. If I can't get to my car, there is a golf cart and an ATV that we used for the event. The golf cart is useless, but the ATV would do nicely, as it has the keys and could easily go across the shallow waters at the falls and follow the creek upstream to the IBC headquarters.

The creek actually goes all the way through town, but the

company headquarters just happen to be to the right of the creek, a few miles shy of the city limits. Probably ten or so miles from here. So if the ATV has enough gas, I can get there in a couple of hours, borrow Carla's pickup truck then maybe crash out there and try to figure out what to do. Stolen money, crooked cops and Nostril Man, not to mention the MDMA, have my head spinning with both knowledge and confusion.

THE WiNE iS LiKE YOUR HAiR

The tank is full, and coasting the ATV conveniently down a small hill is simple. I see Carla and Jack talking intently through the office window. Now, starting the engine and putting it in gear, I proceed unnoticed through the junipers toward the shallow crossing at Honeycomb Falls.

It's a dark night, and I will definitely need the headlights to cut through the small amount of fog coming off the creek. Happily, I managed to escape the office with the remote control and aerosol can of video screen stuff. I put them in a small backpack I find on the four-wheeler then ease through the creek, turning to the left toward IBC. Mr. Cigar is standing on the gas tank, staring straight ahead.

We enter an unknown thicket of ginormous oak trees. I turn on the headlights and what was a forest of substantial oaks becomes a large, well-lit room with tree trunks. The lights have apparently changed my spatial orientation, but not nearly as much, I fear, as the MDMA that Mike the DJ just gave me. Where did that guy even come from? I fully expect to see him at any moment appear from behind a shadow and gleefully offer me a drug-laced candy bar or something.

At a small tributary I'm forced to go away from the main creek to avoid some rocks, and I find myself totally lost.

I crossed that tributary . . . Now I can't find it or where I'm supposed to be, and the shadows are starting to get fuzzy and a little drifty. I wonder if I will ever not feel like this. Then for some reason I turn off the headlights and take the remote control out of the backpack.

THE BEST RAMEN iN TOWN

From what Carla said, I have several hours before Mr. Cigar deactivates (video-wise), so I press the center button of the remote and switch my dog to "light show" heavy on the RAN-DOM. Self-illuminated, he rainbows over the handlebars to the ground, both of us happily barking now. I track his psychedelic movements and confidently follow him through the forest with my headlamps turned off.

Wow, the controller for this thing is amazing—really quick response.

I can eaily make Mr. Cigar a jumble of lights or an orderly pattern . . . my choice. In the light show mode, one can toggle the variation knob back and forth, giving different morph looks every time you switch, thus making the device playble; almost like a musical instrument. When satisfied with a setting you can rotate whatever knob the opposite direction, predictably creating new colors and patterns or returning to previous ones. Hard to describe but oddly intuitive. Typical Carla Marks. Best way to put it is this thing is cool and in only a matter of minutes I've become fairly adept at switching

Mr. Cigar back and forth from light show to Recognize, camouflage and beyond all in a highly predictable manner. This system is super entertaining, and I can see value in this technology beyond intended purpose. Like, I mean, it's just fun to use. I totally grasp the implications of its camouflage feature, which doesn't work quite as well in the dark but beyond that the technology is really too good to be a government secret. I mean, a dog-shaped TV screen? How cool is that? The Recognize feature on Cigar is particularly fun—like I can dial up different dogs and Cigar retains his shape but at the same time becomes a poodle or whatever, and at first he convincingly becomes a poodle, but if I study fairly closely I can tell something is going on. So I guess the technology isn't perfect, but it's good enough to fool most people . . . definitely.

Cigar jumps back and forth from the ATV gas tank to the ground barking, directing and flowing as we make our way upstream toward the IBC properly. The trees are huge in these woods, and the ATV easily chews up the terrain, while the outspread limbs and leaves seem to be pointing the way in this huge green room with a low ceiling and no walls or doors.

I can feel the effects of Mike's water bottle, but they're not nearly as intense as before. Mr. Cigar is all lit up; he keeps alternating riding or leading. Following the stream is almost dreamy . . . even trancelike. Effortless. Fortunately, or not, there is no family of dancing bears this time around. But I can't stop thinking about Colonel Sanders's nostril hole . . . and all of that stuff.

No car, no phone. Crooked cops. Basically riding a stolen vehicle through the woods high on Molly . . . to go steal another vehicle.

Kids these days.

LAST DAYS OF THE ROMANOFFS

CHAPTER 36

I realize there is a certain segment of the population whose daily activities regularly include such things, but it's just not my style. I am at least lucky the clown bust wasn't seen by anybody that matters. I have a few grand in my checking account, so I am by no means broke. We had a significant percentage of the crowd pay at the door tonight, and that money, and more, was in the clown's backpack when he got jumped by the police. That's all gone now.

I guess it's no big deal . . . My parents—or parent—are fucking rich. So, pitiful as it may be, I actually do have a trust fund (from Dad's life insurance). So I'm okay. I wish I could say the same for the Lytle: he never has any money, he drives a beat-up truck (awesome motor) but you can bet he doesn't have a trust fund. In fact, I'm sure he doesn't have a trust fund, because he lives with me or at least most of the time he lives with me—and I would know.

He has the upstairs in the folks' garage apartment. I have the downstairs. I say "most of the time" because three or four days out of the week I end up crashing at Carla's. It's way closer to IBC, plus Carla has an awesome cook. I hardly ever go inside my folks' actual house anymore. It's way too spooky for one person . . . especially at night. My mom is always with her boyfriend, and I get depressed when I'm alone there. It reminds me of my dad and the way things used to be. But Lytle has been my roommate for almost two years, and we have a great time out back.

He's a year older than me. His middle name is Falstaff. Lytle Falstaff. He says I'm the only person in the world he's ever admitted that to and claims even his father doesn't know his middle name. I met him when he was the first person to arrive at one of the first parties in the garage apartment where we now live. He came thirty minutes early, and we just kind of hit it off. His father owned the landscaping business that does my parents' garden and lawn. I say "owned" because his parents broke up and his mom got the business. All his dad got were the boat and the F-350 (at least that's what he tells Lytle and anybody who'll listen), and there's the thirty-year-old Starbucks manager he ran away with too.

His philandering makes Lytle want to vomit, and everybody else thinks it's gross, but Dan's Lawn Services is now Jan's Lawn Services, and that's kind of funny. Funny too that Lytle is the only person besides me, my sister and Larry Teeter who saw what happened that day my sister lost her hand.

THE CHOCOLATE CHAINSAW

He was working for his dad that day. His dad was around back, so only Lytle had a clear view of the incident. He might have been able to see what happened, but I know Lytle doesn't have any idea what really took my sister's hand off. Neither do I. It was a Saturday, and he was thirteen. Also, that day his mom found out about his dad's infidelity with the Starbucks lady, and that night Lytle was in Enid, Oklahoma, at his aunt's house, where he stayed until the divorce was all settled two years later.

When his mom took over the family business, they moved back down to Texas. They were here only for a week when me and Lytle re-met. I was putting some ice in the bathtub when he walked in the front door of the apartment thirty minutes before anyone else. He offered his services and his mother's car for a last-minute ice run, saying, "It's got a Jimmy Dean Martin Landau roof" as we hopped in for the six block-journey.

I thought about that and on the way back, ended a moment of silence with, "I'm glad Elton John Glenn Campbell is DJ'ing tonight."

Ever since . . . that particular style of linking wordplay has become a running tête-à-tête in our everchanging verbal relationship.

Later that night, sporting a total deadpan expression, he wisks up beside me on the dance floor, saying, "I just made out with Bob Hope Lange . . . Older chicks are cool." It still cracks me up. The kid's got talent, what can I say?

Later, he said something like: "Hey, Oscar, you don't know me, but I totally saw that owl thing bite your sister's hand off."

Amazing.

I said, "What are you talking about?"

And he started laughing, a seriously crazy laugh . . . and I started laughing too, and didn't stop. That's pretty much what we still do. We had so much fun that night we started throwing parties together, and now we're roommates and partners in crime as well as business. The sports team at his junior high were the Fighting Owls, and he's told me many times how he got a lot of mileage in high school out of telling people he once saw a girl get her hand bitten off by an owl in Texas.

His mom, Jan, who is awesome and comes over to cook for us like three times a week, says, "Oh, Lytle, you know that was a lawn mower."

Lytle always winks at me when she isn't looking and says, "Well, a lawn mower was there."

But it was no ordinary lawn mower, because it flew up toward the hill country after it bit her hand off. Although I know Mr. Cigar is special, magical or whatever to the outside observer, he is just an ordinary dog. Others may take his behavior as being extremely obedient, while I treat him as an equal. He may not seem so magical to them. I have come to rely on him, I never take him for granted and I think, to a certain degree, he relies on me . . . after all, I never feed him dog food, and he knows I never would. I think to Lytle, Mr. Cigar is a dog. He can tell Cigar is smart but thinks he's just a regular canine.

I think.

Just like me until I saw Mr. Cigar come back from the grave and give birth to a flying bat dog with photo-morphing-skin capabilities.

A TRUNKiE
CORNER

The government contractor totally freaks me out. He definitely and specifically wants Mr. Cigar. I suspect these two have a definite and specific history together. He accused Mr. Cigar of being, of all things, military property. I hope I never find out why. Mr. Cigar belongs to ME.

Pulling the ATV out of a particularly treacherous corner, I notice a light in the eastern sky. So it had to be past six A.M. We've been going fairly steady for a couple of hours now, so for sure we're getting close. At the next bunch of trees I recognize the pecan grove surrounding the company property, then—turning left along the creek—a parking lot, a warehouse and a couple of trucks . . . IBC.

Through the water and up a small hill, I see the vehicle of interest and next to it . . . two familiar cars. Apparently, Carla and Jack came to work early. Oh man. I know somebody noticed the missing ATV and probably figured I took it. So this might be tricky. Not a bad one but definitely "one."

Through the unlocked front door I walk in to find . . . Jack Ogilvie and Carla in the reception area, drinking coffee and watching some black-and-white documentary jazz performance.

Jack waves. Carla notices, turns to me and waves too.

"Hey, guys? Uh . . . what's going on? Seriously."

"Oscar, that was so weird last night," Carla says, her eyes sort of back on the TV. "Are you all right? Well, we figured you were all right. You kept moving."

"What do you mean I kept moving?"

"We were watching you," Jack explains, pointing to a laptop. "The ATV has a beacon that can be initiated remotely. It can be disabled at the vehicle, but it's a hunter's safety option. I thought it was neat . . . Low Jack . . . Get it?!"

I nod. After all, I stole the ATV in question. "That *is* neat."

"It wasn't that expensive, but they sting you on the activation fee."

Carla sniffles. I suddenly realize she's been crying. "I was worried about you, sweetie," she says. "Lytle too. He's still at large. And with the colonel after you—"

"Who the fuck is that guy, anyway?"

Before I can obsess too much over whether or not Lytle has been busted again, Jack Ogilvie fills me in on a little of the colonel's history.

It sort of makes sense, in a less-than-understandable way.

YOU KNOW WHAT TO DO WiTH THE COCONUT

"You see, Oscar, I've known Pete for a long time—we were in basic and combat together as sailors, and he's the kind of guy that you want on your side when the tough gets goin'. But when the tough gets gone, he's . . . really intense. I think he tends to take his job home with him, and he got in more than a couple of fights with fellow soldiers . . . the ones on his side. Nonetheless, he is professional, highly qualified and extremely by the book. It's just that sometimes he wants to be the one who writes the book. But, along with your dad, we met in boot camp, did our first tour together then got different assignments. He went into some MCIA training program, and now he can't talk about a lot of it. I kept flying F-35s and we didn't keep in contact until his name came up in an IBC meeting and I learned he was a military tech acquisition specialist. Sort of the typical IBC customer. Like I said, we didn't keep in contact, but over the years bits and pieces of what Pete did in those five-plus years have come to the surface or at least circulated in hushed tones (among the people in the intelligence community)."

"Wow, Jack, are you going to tell me some classified dirt on Colonel Sanders?"

"Well, maybe. No, not really. Most of what I'm going to say is speakable, but I might include some heretofore redacted information. Heh heh."

I laugh too. "Wow, cool."

He frowns. "No, it's really not that cool."

"Oh."

"It's just that a significant portion of that which has been repeated over the years is so ridiculous that it can't be true. Okay, here it is. They say he was working on a classified program that somehow involved wildlife or animals. These type of operations aren't unusual—from carrier pigeons to even trained dolphins. The military has been using animals in all sorts of ways for years. Apparently, in Pete's case, the animal he was involved with attacked him and escaped. That much is fairly undisputed. In fact, it almost tore off his nose and actually fully severed two fingers. Obviously, he's got the scars to prove something. They say the animal was never recovered and the program got shut down. What they don't say is what kind of animal it was. It's certain he was working at a canine research facility in North Texas. I had a layover at Sheppard AFB almost twenty years ago and ran into him there. We had a few minutes to catch up, and he told me he was still working for the MCIA. When I asked what his mission was, he winked and kind of laughingly said, 'Right now we're training dogs.' Then he changed the subject. Sounded reasonable to me . . . I thought it was probably part of a bigger project and left it at that. Like I said, that was almost twenty years ago. Next time I saw him was last year, when he turned up as a purchasing rep buying IBC technology."

Jack Ogilvie pauses.

"So, what's the weird part?" I ask.

"Well, Oscar, the weird part is that a few years back I got a call from a friend who had served with me and Colonel Sanders in Indonesia. He said he ran into Pete the night after he got out of the hospital from the animal attack. They went out to dinner, and over some drinks Pete told him a weird tale indeed. Basically Colonel Sanders told our mutual buddy that an immortal dog with telepathic powers had maimed him and run off into the North Texas countryside. Rich, our mutual buddy, said Pete looked him right in the eye and said, 'That goddamn commie dog nearly tore my nose off.' At this point, Rich said he convulsed with laughter, saying, 'I understand the immortal, telepathic part, but why is the dog a communist?' He said Pete didn't crack a smile and said, 'Because Khrushchev gave the damn thing to Kennedy.' He also told Rich he had seen a tintype photograph of the dog sitting on the lap of Grigori Rasputin."

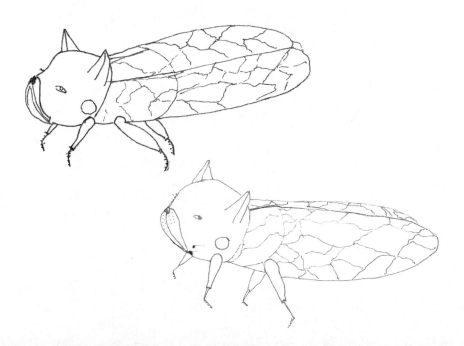

"Wow, man."

"I know. Rich might have just blamed it on the drinks—apparently, they'd had a few—but over the next few years the stories kept coming back around . . . and from different sources. Everybody felt bad for Pete, but you can't say stuff like that and keep a career in the US military . . . even if it is true. So, needless to say, the program got canceled or redirected, and Pete retired from the navy. Or was forced to resign. Which is a lot more likely . . . if you believe the stories."

APOLLO STATION ZEBRA

This whole time Mr. Cigar has been sitting next to me, intently staring at Jack. I catch his eye, and I swear he winks at me then continues his gaze.

"So what you're saying is that you think that guy from last night thinks that Mr. Cigar is an immortal clairvoyant dog given to John F. Kennedy by the leader of the Soviet Union."

"Well, yes, but the salient piece is that he's upset because Mr. Cigar ruined his career. As well as almost tearing his nose off. Ouch."

Holy shit, I'm thinking, so that's who/what Mr. Cigar really is.

I shake my head. In spite of the drugs, I still can maintain a standard of reality. "I gotta say, guys, that story just doesn't make any sense. I mean, why in the name of logic, if you had a clairvoyant immortal dog, would you possibly want to give it away?"

Cigar barks.

Carla laughs. "Exactly."

Jack laughs too.

We all laugh.

I stop when Cigar springs from the couch and runs to the door. He jerks his nose at me and barks three more times—loudly—then shoves the door open. Looking toward the facility entrance, I see two blacked-out sedans entering the parking lot.

"Oh no, you guys. It looks like Colonel Sanders is back to get Cigar."

"'Oh no' is right, Oscar," Carla says in a shaky voice. Then, quickly recovering: "I'm sure the colonel is fairly harmless, but I don't want a repeat of the after-party scene, so here . . . Here are the keys to the white truck in the back. But at some point, I really need to talk with you, okay? Your mother called. She is going to stay in Florida for a few days."

"I don't know why she doesn't call you," Carla wonders. "So take the truck to my place. Go . . . I'll see you down at the guesthouse after; we'll all get some sleep."

Our eyes meet. I force a smile. "Cool, Carla. Thanks for the truck." I pause. "I probably would have taken it anyway."

Carla smiles back, her eyes damp. "I know, sweetie."

THE WAY-OUT CAT NAMED WiLLiE

Down the hall, past the lab, to the loading dock. This place is kind of creepy with no one here. Off-hours lighting is supplied by one of Carla's crazy solar inventions. It lends a cool blue glow/essence to the entire facility. I slip out the back into the pickup truck, down the driveway to the rear entrance of IBC . . . then home. Well . . . sort of home—to Carla's house with Mr. Cigar. Maybe sleep. MDMA still tugging at my psyche as we autopilot south on the interstate toward FM26. That's 26 . . . 2 x 13—double unlucky, I'm thinkin', then, glancing over to the passenger side, I notice that Mr. Cigar has managed to bring my little drawstring backpack containing my dead iPhone, the aerosol can and the remote control. Maybe not so unlucky after all. I need my cell phone, and the light-show camouflage unit is just plain cool.

Nice job, Cigar.

Finally to Carla's house.

I pull into the guesthouse garage, make my way upstairs, plug in my smart-ass phone and collapse on the couch.

AFFORDING A CADILLAC

CHAPTER 42

I instantly pass out, dreaming of nothing. Mr. Cigar is a warm ball on my stomach doing whatever he does when I'm asleep. After what seems like minutes, I wake to Mr. Cigar standing on my chest and the sound of pre–Henry Rollins Black Flag coming from behind my head. It's Lytle's ringtone—as far from opera as humanly possible. Lytle loves opera. I hate it.

"Hey, Lytle."

"Where you been, man? It's almost four o'clock in the afternoon! I just left your folks' house. I've been trying to call you since noon. We got to figure out what to do about that freaky cop."

I rub my eyes. Cigar hops down, and I sit up. "Sorry, man, I was totally passed out . . . I'm at Carla's house, and you're not going to believe what happened last night."

"Yeah, I can! We had a cool party going on, you disappeared and we got our shit jacked by some Texas Ranger–wannabe douche named Cletus Acox!"

I laugh hoarsely. "No, not that part, man. After that . . . you left and I went to the trailer to talk to Carla and some government agent dude with a ripped-up nostril bum-rushes me and tries to steal Mr. Cigar."

Lytle pauses. "Wuh?"

"Yep, and I left my car at the gig and drove the ATV through the woods to get to IBC so I could borrow their truck and get home."

"Cool."

I shake my head. "No, not cool . . . and when I got there, Nostril Man, whose name is Colonel Sanders, was basically waiting for us."

"Wow, Colonel Sanders? I haven't eaten all day—"

Mr. Cigar cuts him off. Interrupts with three familiar crisp, loud barks. Oh, shit. Out the window and up the driveway I see two blacked-out sedans coming onto the property. Inside. The security gate shuts behind them.

"Where are you, Lytle?"

"I'm like five minutes from Carla's driveway, dude. At the bottom of the hill on 26 just behind her property. I can fucking see the garage roof from here—"

"Stay right there. I'll be there in one minute."

I grab my backpack and a toothbrush and dash out the back door, down the hill to Lytle's car.

X GAMES

Halfway down, Cigar pulls up next to me and glances up. He is taking effortlessly huge strides, looking up at me while carrying my backpack in his mouth. We make it to the open door of Lytle's pickup. I hop in—Cigar on my lap—close the door and we're gone.

"Oh my God, dude, what's going on?"

"Just keep going straight, man . . . This is crazy. Those cars—I mean, the Colonel Sanders dude just pulled into Carla's driveway. That guy wants Cigar. Bad man . . . He's chasing me wicked-style. We got a bunch of shit to figure out. We can't go to my mom's house, man. I know they'll go there if they haven't already."

Lytle grips the wheel, scowling. "Why would Colonel Sanders want Mr. Cigar? And what are 'those cars'?"

"Because he thinks Cigar is an immortal clairvoyant dog from nineteenth-century Russia. Those are the blacked-out box-shaped sedans they drive. They look like fucking robots."

Finally, Lytle cracks a grin. "I could have told you that about Mr. Cigar, dude. But how many cars?"

"Two . . . why?"

"Because earlier there were two blacked-out box-shaped sedans parked in front of your mom's place."

"Wait, what? When?"

"They were there just after noon, when I woke up, and when I left they were gone. Don't know when they left . . . but . . ."

"I get it. We can't go there, we can't go to Carla's, we . . ." My brain sputters to a stop.

"Let's just go to my mom's house and chill out. I know she's home, plus I'm starved." He shoots me a glance out of the corner of his eye. "Chicken-fried steak?"

"Yep." All at once, I feel better. "I love your mom's chicken-fried steak. Sweet."

HANDS UP ...
WHO WANTS
TO DiE?

Chicken-fried steak: a dish in which a crappy piece of meat is beaten and battered and fried like chicken till it's golden brown; asphyxiated with creamy gravy then served with mashed potatoes and some kind of greens. It's awesome. It gives you diarrhea, and it was invented in the southern part of the Great Plains, in the Panhandle region of Texas. Lytle reminds me it's the state dish of Oklahoma, and I remind him the reason that Texas doesn't float off into the Gulf of Mexico is that Oklahoma sucks. He says Texas sucks back, and then we agree that chicken-fried steak was probably invented in Colorado anyway.

So, the chicken-fried steak is stunning. I finish off my second serving, brace for diarrhea, then collapse onto the couch, Mr. Cigar in the crook of my knee, with the TV show *Cops Reloaded* flickering away on Lytle's mom's TV screen. Then I awake to the sound of British air raid sirens.

My sister, Rachel's, ringtone.

THE CALL
OF THE WILD

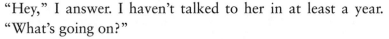

"Hey," I answer. I haven't talked to her in at least a year. "What's going on?"

"Oh, Oscar, I'm sorry to call so early, but I really, really need your help."

"Why, what is it?"

"Well, Oscar, I kinda got in a, uh . . . You remember JJ, right?"

"Yeah, your creepy ex. What? What did he do?"

"He didn't do anything. Back when we were going out I loaned him five thousand dollars one time."

"Yeah?"

"And I kind of, not really, got involved in some stuff because—"

"What?"

"Listen, he used the money to pay back his cousin, who's an asshole. His name is Ricky and he found out where JJ got the money, so now he thinks I'm rich and can pay JJ's . . . whatever. Debt."

"Rachel, you *are* rich."

She groans. "I know. He thinks I'm liquid rich, though. I live in a seven-thousand-dollar-a-month apartment and have six thousand dollars in my checking account, and my show next—"

"Yeah, yeah, yeah, what does the asshole cousin want?"

"He's got JJ and wants thirty-five thousand dollars."

"What? He kidnapped JJ and wants thirty-five thousand dollars' ransom? Call the FBI, jeez! Thirty-five thousand?"

"No, it's not like that."

"What do you mean it's not like that?"

"Well . . ."

"Well, what?"

"Well, basically . . . if he gets busted, JJ and I get busted . . . but . . ."

"But what? Oh man, are you okay?"

"Yeah, I'm okay and JJ's okay. He's not really getting kidnapped, but I kind of promised him . . . them . . . the money, and I can pay you back. It's not that big of a deal. But, Oscar, I need thirty-five thousand, and all I have is six thousand."

"Oh. Not that big a deal? And you promised him? What does that mean?"

"I know, I know . . . I know it sounds totally weird, but I need thirty-five thousand dollars, and I know you're the richest teenager in Texas."

"Oh, shut up!"

"And you had a party the other night. You always tell me how much you make at your parties. Please, Oscar! Please!"

"I'm not—"

Click.

WTF? I call her back. It goes straight to voice mail.

THE INVENTOR
OF BACON

Lying there waiting for her to call back, my head is spinning. Government agents. Crooked cops. Quasi-kidnapping. New York City street hassle thingy. I don't know. And on top of that, a much deeper understanding of Mr. Cigar, who is sitting on my chest licking my neck.

I try to call my sister again; it goes straight to voice mail.

I text her to call me when Lytle walks into the living room wearing purple knee-length satin boxing shorts and a Carlos Santana T-shirt.

"Hey, man, you passed out last night mid-*Cops*. You didn't even make it to *Locked Up Abroad*." He yawns and stretches. "What's going on? Who called? There were sirens, and I heard you say, 'Whaaaat?' real loud."

"Oh, dude. It was my sister . . . She's in some freaky situation with her ex and needs thirty-five thousand dollars."

"Whoa, dude . . . Just thirty-five thousand? Ha ha. I thought your sister was a stylin' NYC artist? She's got a sick pad. What's the dealio?"

"You're not going to believe it, but the way she's describing it, it sounds like ransom for a kidnapping. But the police can't be involved."

Lytle nods. "Well, yeah, I can dig that."

"Yeah, no shit. We got disconnected and it's been straight to voice mail for the last twenty minutes."

"She'll call back, man. Let's get something to eat."

"Sure, man. Where do you want to go?"

"Mom's kitchen."

"Sweet."

Lytle turns on the TV. As bacon gently sizzles on the stove, a text pings. I look at my phone. CALLER UNKNOWN. The message ominously reads: *BRING THE CASH TO YOUR SISTER'S APT. FRIDAY AFTERNOON! DON'T BE A FOOL.*

Holy . . . shit. That doesn't sound like my sister, unless she's turned into a wacko prankster with low-level tech skills. I think she might actually be in trouble and need my help.

The only things certain that I got from her story were that she needs thirty-five thousand dollars. And: *no cops!* I'm only about eighteen thousand short and fifteen hundred miles away. I know I could drive there in thirty hours, and I know I owe my sister. But I don't know where to get thirty-five grand. We got ripped off at the gig. I've got maybe seventeen grand in my checking account.

"Lytle?"

"Yeah, man?"

"You know your uncle who you always say we should do business with, but then we always agree he's too shady to consider?"

"Jimbo?"

"Do you think Jimbo might be able to turn a quick deal?"

"What kind of deal?" Lytle asks.

"I don't know. One where we can double our money in a simple flip kind of deal."

"Oh, that one . . . Why?"

I stare at my phone. "I think my sister's situation is a tad more serious than I first realized . . . We need to bring her thirty-five grand, and we need to be there by Friday, apparently."

"Wait a second. We? Friday? Bring? Deal? Jimbo? Wow, dude. I'm in!" Lytle's voice drips with sarcasm.

"No, seriously. Dude—"

"No, seriously, I'm in," he interrupts, standing right in front of me. "This'll look great on the résumé. Do you really think she's in harm's way?"

"I don't know if she's in trouble for sure, but for sure she needs money. She's never asked me for anything like this, and I feel like I owe her . . . I mean my dog . . . the lawn mower . . ."

"Yeah, the lawn mower that can fly," Lytle says. "You crack me up, man."

"Likewise. Call Jimbo. See what he says."

"Cool, man. Calling Jimbo."

A CARROT FROM THE WHEELCHAIR GUY

Rachel's phone now goes directly to a temporarily-out-of-order message. Lytle protests as the TV goes from an old Western to a radar view of the North Texas area. A thunderstorm is rolling in from the north, and the National Weather Service reveals a huge squall line extending from the Panhandle to Texarkana. The storm is heading our way. I look outside: the sky is crazy. Divided by an enormous looming wall. One half is partly cloudy and sunny. The other half is a green vertical sea of boiling thunderclouds. They are hundreds of miles away, perhaps, but they're so tall it looks like they're next door.

Finally, the annoying emergency weather beeping signal gives way to a broadcaster warning that numerous funnel clouds have been observed across the entire North Texas region, yet there are no reports that any have hit the ground. Back to the normally scheduled program . . . a killer episode of *Bonanza*. I love this weather, and I love *Bonanza*. Both used to scare me when I was a little kid, and they still do. It's just nowadays I sort of look forward to being scared . . . Now Hoss, cradling a bouquet of flowers, enthusiastically announces to Candy that he's going into town and he's "takin' the wagon." Candy chuckles a "wow" then nods his approval. Just then Lytle walks into the living room from the front porch and howls at the notion of Hoss-sex in the Wild West. He then looks at me, waving his phone. "We're in business."

"The weather is so fry-king cool, man," proclaims Lytle. "I just talked to Jimbo, and it's totally on."

"Wow, you said 'Fry King.' I get it. But . . . totally on?"

"Well, Jimmy has a 'friend' who happens to have a large amount of totally bangin' Cali," Lytle said.

"Did you just say 'totally bangin' Cali'?"

"Yes, I did. Totally bangin' Cali that we can get for two grand a pound."

"Cool. And what do we do with pounds of totally bangin' Cali? Sell it in totally tiny bags for the rest of our tiny lives?"

"I get you, man. But no. First of all, he is the friend with the large amount of weed."

"I suspected as much."

"And he knows a guy we can turn around and sell it to for four grand a pound."

I shake my head, dubious. "If he knows a guy we can sell it to, why doesn't he just do it himself? That's why he has a large amount of totally bangin' Cali. Right?"

"I know, dude, but here's the answer. It's not that the guy is untrustworthy, it's just that Jimbo doesn't trust the situation."

"This is really starting to not make sense now . . . So if Jimbo doesn't trust him, why should we?"

"You're asking the same questions I did, Oscar. He doesn't know the guy, but he knows *of* him. He knows that he's *the* weed guy for all the kids in Shady Oaks."

I have a brief, unpleasant memory of Sergeant Cletus Acox. "Shady Oaks . . . now, that part makes sense. Jimbo lives in Shady Oaks, dude."

"I know, I know, but everybody knows everybody in Shady Oaks, and the other day the weed guy cold-called Jimmy at his apartment wanting to buy some weed and it kind of freaked ol' Jimbo out. He's always said he'd never do business with anyone in his own neighborhood. So that's one reason he won't trust the guy. But another reason, and I think it's the main reason, is because the weed dude is white."

"Ah ha ha ha ha ha."

"Yep, but you know the weed dude. It's Larry Teeter."

"Oh, wow . . . You're kidding me!"

"Nope. He gave Jimbo his number, so all you gotta do is call up Larry, and bam, we're in business."

"That might work, man," I say. "I saw him the afternoon of the gig. He seemed friendly. I could actually just go knock on his door . . ."

"Cool, man. You don't have to. Just call him up. Jimbo gave me his number and I'll call Jimbo to set it up."

RUDE
AiR-CONDiTiONiNG

The weather finally hit town. The temperature dropped like thirty degrees, then there was crazy lightning, exploding thunder and sideways rain, turning now to a major hailstorm pummeling the metal roof of Lytle's mom's house, sounding like a giant oak tree slowly getting snapped at the trunk . . . for like ten straight minutes. The storm is relentless. Then it stops.

The green clouds open to the west and a silver-blue skyline delivers amazing yellow horizontal light. Crispy sunshine accentuates the hailstones, now a solid white bumpy layer, everywhere.

Despite the storm's passing, it continues to deliver gentle rainfall. A sun shower, if you will. In the southern United States, and apparently in Hungary as well, when this phenomena presents itself they say, "The devil is beating his wife." A truly awesome expression, however perplexing. After all, why would the devil feel the need to tie the knot anyway, did a clergyman perform the ceremony and what in God's name does the devil's wife look like? Well, apparently even devils need love, it could have been one of those Internet preachers and, whatever the devil's wife looks like, she must be hot. The oddly dry cold air feels great. Three cars in front of Lytle's house have shattered windows and car alarms are sounding all over the neighborhood. To go from ninety-something and humid to seventy and dry was awesome. I love Texas weather. Lytle calls his uncle. I call Larry. Jimbo is waiting for the word, and Larry answers his phone.

"Hey, Larry . . . You're never going to believe this, but this is Oscar."

"Wow, dude. This is kind of weird. How did you get my number, man? What's up?"

"Well, it's kind of a trip, Larry," I begin. "See, I know Jimbo . . ."

After that I tell him a bunch of lies, and he agrees to the transaction. We're set to do the deal around 10 o'clock tonight at his Shady Oaks apartment—on our way out of town.

TCB

Jimbo is on his way. Larry's waiting for us too. Backing out of the carport in Lytle's pickup, I see that the steam created by the hailstones and the humidity is making a weird optical fog, maybe six feet in the air, with wisps rising higher, making an occasional circular rainbow over the sun. Crazy. All I have to do now is run by the bank, grab some of Lytle's clothes (they fit me), get the weed from Jimbo and head out west to Shady Oaks . . . then meet Larry, do the deal, and get on the Interstate.

We'll have a little over thirty-five grand with a projected arrival time in NYC of early Thursday morning. My sister's phone continues to go straight to VM. No answers to my texts.

THE INCREDIBLY FANTASTIC JOURNEY VOYAGE

The bank run goes smoothly, and walking into the house I can tell instantly that Jimbo has already arrived. The air is thick with the unmistakable odor of high-quality pot. They don't call it skunkweed for nothing. Jimbo appears out of Lytle's room and I say, "Smells like a good deal, man."

As I hand him the cash, he's laughing. We shake hello, goodbye, and thanks. He waves back at us on his way out the front door, a smile on his face and a pocket full of bills.

Lytle throws together enough clothes for the two of us, and I grab my backpack, which contains a toothbrush, an aerosol can, and a wireless remote control. Doesn't sound that impressive, but it is an astonishingly powerful package to carry around like some schoolbooks. Not to mention my additional secret weapon—Mr. Cigar, another powerful package indeed. And so stealthy, no one would know what either of them really is. The last sliver of the sun is disappearing in the western skyway, way past Fort Worth.

We're stepping out the front door of Lytle's mom's house as it dawns on me: the insanity of this journey. I love Lytle, and we have done some fairly impossible things together, so I believe he knows what he's in for and what he's capable of. Plus, he's pumped, and we're probably going to have a great time. And double plus, we're taking his pickup truck.

He claims it's indestructible. Ugly but sturdy . . . or . . . butt-ugly sturdy . . . with a killer stereo. Now we just have to sell the weed to Larry Teeter.

TRANSPARENT RADIATION

I keep asking myself if this is truly crazy, but she *is* my sister. I've never been on a real road trip. Plus, a weird Blackwater-CIA guy wants my dog, and I gotta blow town for a while. No big deal. I'll see my sister and come back in a few days, at least until I get the high sign from Carla that Nostril Man isn't on the prowl anymore. I'm looking forward to not looking over my shoulder.

Maybe the MDMA from the other night is affecting my judgment, because I'm actually looking forward to the trip, and I feel great. I had a great dinner last night. I didn't have diarrhea and slept for like thirteen hours. Lytle's truck used to be one of the landscaping company's work trucks, and it has this fold-out plywood thing for equipment in the back seat. It makes a great bed, so we'll be able to drive basically nonstop. I drive while Lytle sleeps and Mr. Cigar DJs. When Lytle wakes up, we go to a Waffle House, then he drives while I sleep. Hopefully we'll get to NYC before Mr. Cigar has to drive and Lytle DJs. Opera gives me the hives.

I hate opera, which is what Lytle listens to if he's not off in IDM land.

It is a cloudless, crisp evening for this time of year. The moon is coming up bright into a blue-black sky. The shadows are heavy, but the night seems optimistic.

We pull off down Third Street to MLK Boulevard, NYC-bound with two dudes, one dog and a cardboard box the size of a large ice chest filled with one-pound bags of gigantic stinky buds of California marijuana. So stinky we put a tarp over it. A futile attempt to hide the acrid smell. It's hard-core. We might as well have just hit a skunk. But Lytle's mom's house is not too far from Shady Oaks, where Larry lives.

It's funny, I suspect our pot just came down this same road. Only it was headed *our* way then. Everything is going to be cool.

i AM GiNA'S KiDNEY

About halfway there in the wooded hollow right before Catfish Creek (where you're more likely to catch a washing machine than a catfish), there's a police car on the side of the road. Halfway across the bridge, just past the cop, I sneak a look back. He's pulled out onto the road and turned on his lights. The cab of the pickup is suddenly filled with red flashing lights. For some reason the *thump-thump-thump* of the metal slats on the bridge is particularly loud tonight. I pull the truck over, stick it in park and look over at Lytle and Mr. Cigar. Wide-eyed, we simultaneously mouth an elongated *Ohhhh shiiiiit*. We are totally fucked if this cop has half a nose.

As he walks up to the driver's side I notice an odd yet familiar smirk on his face. Leaning into the window, eyeing both Lytle and me, he tells me to turn off the ignition and asks for our IDs.

Then he turns toward the rear of the pickup and says in a smart-ass voice, "What do ya got in the back?"

He steps away to take a look. Lytle and I let out another

simultaneous, "Oh, shit!" This time it's audible. There's a silent mutual realization: That's him!

"Dude," Lytle whispers. "That's the dude, the cop that stole our money at the party."

"I know who he is," I grumble. "The cop who hassled me in Shady Oaks. Before the party, right after I picked up the balloon candy. He knew my name. Creeps me out."

"Dude, this is totally a setup."

"Fucking Cletus Acox," we both say.

"Thank Larry Teeter." I scowl in the rearview. "Look at those sideburns, dude . . ."

Mr. Cigar has been maintaining a low growl the entire time. Suddenly he jumps into my lap and cracks out a sharp, singular bark.

From the back of the truck, Sergeant Cletus lets out a whoop. "Hoo-boy . . . Lookie there!" He lifts up the tarp that covers the weed, then fake chokes, grinning ominously. "That smells craaazeee . . . heh heh."

He returns to my window, and Mr. Cigar lunges slightly toward him, growling in a heightened manner.

"Watch your dog, now," Acox warns. Pausing, he moves his hand toward his hip and stares eye to eye with Mr. Cigar . . . right at the moment his hand comes in contact with a Smith & Wesson .38-caliber revolver. Completely in harm's way, with a deceptive amount of skill, craft and power, Mr. Cigar makes his leaping move.

All hell breaks loose, and a gun goes off.

THE PEANUT, THE CHICKEN AND THE THUNDERCLOUD

For about as long as it's mattered, I've had Mr. Cigar as a partner. After my sister's . . . uh . . . injury, he's never left my side. During her recovery, I was basically alone in the house as my mom and dad, along with a nurse and later a physical therapist, gave her, deservedly, most of their time and attention. In those months, I learned the magic of my new friend, but my sister insisted then, and probably would today, that Mr. Cigar had something to do with the "lawn mower incident" and that some weird flying creature bit off her hand.

It was only after more than a couple of therapy sessions she finally admitted that perhaps she had suffered some form of hallucinatory shock and a swooping owl or hawk had startled her into falling in front of the lawn mower. I still feel bad about the whole thing. However, after only a few years, my sister has clearly become elevated by the accident/incident. Nonetheless, she's always eyed Cigar suspiciously, and they've definitely never bonded. Post incident, Mr. Cigar always went to school with me, either by sneaking onto the school bus or just running through the woods and beating us there when my parents would drive me. People got used to seeing us together, and a sort of playful rumor circulated that he was my twin brother who'd died at birth. Little did they know.

Mr. Cigar has become less like a partner and more like an arm or even a set of lungs. If I need him to be human—even superhuman almost—he's there. I've never seen him sniff another dog's butt (or his own, for that matter) but seen him get in fights when another dog tries to sniff his. That little guy runs as fast as physics allows with those short little legs, blindingly quick, and his jaws could probably bite a two-by-four in half. His overall strength is fairly impressive as well. I don't know if I've ever really felt his full force in any way, but he's powerful to say the least. Not vampire strong, but strong-guy strong. Mr. Cigar definitely has kind of a crazy job. Plus, he's really good at it.

And on this particular night, he was stellar—a cool prairie wind had blown in from the Rocky Mountains and the rain-cleansed air felt almost statically charged.

NUDITY, EXTREME SEX AND STRONG VIOLENT CONTENT

The roadside drainage ditch is basically filled to the top with rainfall rushing downstream to nearby Catfish Creek, where the dank still-water air has been reset to zero. What usually smells like an unflushed toilet is now, if only temporarily, a rather pleasant experience. The grove of crepe myrtles near the creek have been agitated by the brief flood, and the scent of grape bubblegum mixed with your grandmother's pillow permeates the air. Tomorrow morning, it might smell like a mixture of nothing and your grandfather's pillow. Tonight, however, the air is washed and sweet. Then the crazy-loud drone of all things creek bottom goes silent. Gunshot echoing down the gully. The only sound for a breath or two is the gently flowing creek runoff and the dull reverberation of a work shoe skidding across the asphalt.

Then hell continues its quest to escape from the nether regions as Sergeant Cletus Acox screams out, "Goddamn it, that dog made me shoot off my brand-new Red Wing!" as he rolls to his back, clutching at his ankle and screaming louder and louder in pain.

"Goddamn it, I shot off my whole fuckin' foot! Goddamn it, goddamn it, goddamn it!" he continues. He sits up and stares squarely at us and says, "Get me a tourniquet," then passes out.

Π-HEDRAL SURFACE IN QUASI-QUASI-SPACE

"Holy shit, this is so fucked. What do we do?" Lytle half screams.

"Get him a tourniquet?" I say.

"Cool, man. Cool, man," Lytle mumbles, looking around. "Use your belt," he says.

"I don't even wear a belt, man. You ever see me with a belt? Let's use your belt."

"I don't wear a belt either," responds Lytle.

"Yeah, no shit. I'm gonna have to use one of your T-shirts."

We all three spring from the pickup as Lytle mournfully says, "Oh man."

"It's only a T-shirt, dude."

"No, man, it's not the T-shirt. This is gonna be gross."

"Yep," I say.

As we approach Sergeant Acox, Lytle sees the blood and immediately throws up. "Oh man," I say mournfully, then loop the T-shirt around his leg, tie a knot and begin winding it tightly with the help of the Maglite I found on Acox's belt.

"Is it working?" asks Lytle. The bleeding is way down. "I can't look, man. We gotta call 911."

"No, don't call 911, use the radio in the squad car. Or just do whatever you want and tell them a cop's gun accidentally discharged and shot him in the foot."

Lytle, with his phone in hand, is staring at something on the other side of the truck. I hear him say, "Wow!"

He continues, "Yeah, yeah, yeah, but check it out! Look at your dog."

"Lytle, call 911!"

"Okay, okay, man."

Mr. Cigar has removed the weed out of the truck and dragged it to the drainage ditch, and it's already about half-way to the creek, slowly taking on water.

Did my dog really just do that? A shame about the weed.

"Hello, 911?"

Lytle continues talking to the operator and walks toward the squad car, clearly following their directions. He opens the trunk, pulls something out and returns. He puts down the phone and says, "Look what I found in the sergeant's trunk." In one hand he has a first-aid kit and in the other, his now-empty backpack Acox stole at the party the other night. Opening the first-aid kit, he finds a real tourniquet, but unable to look at the carnage, he stares into the street while handing me the goods.

"Thanks, man."

"No problem," he replies. "I have an idea," he continues.

I add the new tourniquet higher up on the leg while Lytle runs into the field and grabs a bale of hay and drags it to the truck. After wrestling it into the bed, he covers it with the tarp. As he walks back to me, he kicks the road clear of the scattered pieces of alfalfa that shook loose from the bale.

"Like nothing ever happened," Lytle says. He pauses, listening. The approaching sirens are louder now. "They'll be here in like two minutes. Let's tell 'em we came down here to get a bale of hay for my mother's chicken coop and we got pulled over by this asshole and he freaked out and shot himself."

"Wow, dude, that actually works. We confess to stealing two dollars' worth of hay—for your mom, no less. Only it actually cost us fifteen grand. This was such a setup! Acox is a fucking asshole thief. Either you, JJ, or Larry or Mr. Cigar. And I know it wasn't you, JJ or Cig. Fucking Larry Teeter."

"Yep," chirps Lytle. "Teeter and Acox are a team."

"Exactly."

Cigar barks in agreement.

THE KING JAMES VERSION

As an ambulance and squad car pull up to us, the wounded cop regains consciousness and looks groggily up at Lytle. "Where did you get that backpack, goddamn it? I shot my fucking foot off . . ." And then he passes out again.

A typically chubby cop with a surprisingly mellow demeanor pops out of the squad car and says, "What the hell happened here? They told me a sergeant of mine shot himself and two fellas gave him a hand. How are ya, Acox?"

As the EMT begins an initial evaluation of the injury, the wounded officer weakly raises his head and replies, "Okay . . . fuck, it hurts. Do I have a . . . ahh, fuck, it hurts."

"Okay, now shut up, son. Lie down and let them do their job. I bet it hurts, but you're okay. Thank God—you could have been alone and bled to death. Let me find out what's going on. All right, guys, come on over to my car. Let me get your names and everything."

Walking into the light of his squad car, we come into full view. The slightly alarmed policeman remarks, "Oh lordy, you boys are young. Excuse me, ma'am"—he motions to the

EMS tech—"can you get us something to wipe my sergeant's blood off of this young man's body?" Looking at us, he says, "Goodness gracious, that is gross. I tell you what, this sure was an unfortunate situation, but I sure am glad you fellas were around to do what you did. The dispatcher told me you used your own T-shirt as a tourniquet? I imagine that was fairly intense?"

"Yes, sir. We were . . ." both Lytle and I blurt out, interrupting each other.

"Okay, okay, just one at a time now. First let's get your IDs and just go from the beginning of how y'all pulled over on the side of the road and wound up with your T-shirt tied around the shot-up foot of a Hill County police officer."

I realize at this point that we have gone from being drug dealers to kind of like teenage do-gooders. Dare I say heroes? Oddly satisfying.

We manage to paint a fairly innocent picture. We admit to stealing a bale of hay. I say "stealing," but the hay had been rained on and was probably worth a dollar a bale. We admit to it and Sheriff Podus doesn't flinch. Then, in response to my last name, he asks, "Is that Junior?"

"Well, actually it's The Third," I reply.

"You're Gerry Lester's boy?"

"Yes, sir."

He flashes a melancholy smile. "I knew him a bit from security we provided for Ms. Carla Marks over at IBC. That sure was a shame about his accident, son—he seemed like a really good man."

"Yes, sir. I miss him," I say as the EMT closes the back door to the ambulance.

A groggy Acox says, "They have a truck full of marijuana, and that dog made me shoot off my foot—"

"Quiet, now," The EMT soothes, urging him to calm down.

Sheriff Podus says, "Oh, Sergeant, I think you mistook marijuana for hay. Or rather, I think you mistook hay for marijuana." He strides over to the back of Lytle's pickup and lifts the tarp. "Yep, hay." Then he walks to the ambulance. "It's okay, son. You're gonna be okay, but we gotta figure out how your weapon came out of its holster and discharged itself. State regulations say we have to do an investigation. So, when you're feeling better, we can get a statement. You know the drill." He looks toward me. "I'm looking forward to hearing how your dog did this. How much does your dog weigh? Twenty pounds? Heh heh."

We both smile as the ambulance pulls away into a gathering of fog.

The cop sighs. "Well, boys, like I said, any time a weapon is drawn, there has to be an investigation. Normally, we would go down to the precinct and interview you guys immediately, but that takes forever, and I want to get home. Plus, I know both of you from your parents. I've known Lytle's dad for years. He's had the city hall landscaping contract as long as I've been with Hill County. I think I've seen Lytle mowing the grass in front of PD headquarters on Third Street. Am I right, son?"

"Yes, sir," Lytle replies.

"Heh heh. Sometimes you had a blond Mohawk or a red flattop. Now you're all normal. The only way I recognized you is from the sign on your truck. Anyway, y'all can go now, but I've got to send someone over tomorrow to get a statement with your parents in attendance."

"Um, my mom is in Florida right now, and she won't be back until next week," I say.

"That should be no problem. We can do it all next week. It's going to take Sergeant Acox several days anyway. Jeez, it looked like he blew at least two of his toes off. I looked all around with my flashlight and didn't see any." Then, motioning down with his Maglite in the general area surrounding the incident, Sheriff Podus freezes the beam toward the left rear tire of Lytle's truck. "Oh lordy. There's his shoe. Ooooh. I hope there's nothing inside there."

He reaches in with his foot leaning down a bit and kicks the damaged shoe into the light. It rolls over twice, and out tumbles an unidentifiable two-inch-square piece of bloody human flesh. "Oh, ow, ah." We all cringe out loud.

"Oh man," bemoans the sheriff while eyeing the carnage, then the flowing water in the nearby drainage ditch. "That doesn't look like a keeper, now, does it, fellas?"

THE MENGER SPONGE

There is total silence as Lytle and I drive away from the scene and over Catfish Creek toward Lytle's mom's house. Finally out of sight from the flashing cruisers and tow truck, we erupt.

"Wooooooow, dude. Whoaaaa. That was insane. I'll never sleep again. Somebody blind me. I can't believe what I saw."

Mr. Cigar barks while Lytle and I blurt out weird snippets of what just transpired. For sure that was a setup. Either Larry Teeter's phone was bugged or he and Cletus Acox were in on it together. You could tell he knew we had weed in the truck. He didn't just accidentally pull us over and—blam! It was "accidentally" the kid he ripped off at the party *with* the kid whose name he "mysteriously" knew in the Shady Oaks apartments. Plus Larry Teeter mysteriously appeared by accident five seconds after he let me go. And Larry was just a little too nice. Then we've been dealing with the craziest shit that ever happened to mankind, so we're hours late to deliver the weed and no call from Larry. Hmm. For sure Acox and Teeter are a team. Larry's phone isn't bugged. But we are wildly ecstatic, completely freaked out and totally broke. Feels good.

I say "broke" . . . We have maybe sixteen hundred dollars in cash for travel expenses. Enough.

We pass the cheesy used-car place and in three miles we're either going straight to Lytle's mom's house or left on I-20 toward New York City and my sister.

Realistically, we can't do anything for my sister without money, but I kind of want to make sure she's okay. She's really never sounded this weird before. I bet if my dad was still around, he'd be halfway there (to NYC) in his BMW by now. He definitely wouldn't have Cletus Acox's blood under his fingernails, but he'd go see what was happening with his daughter.

I'm going, but I don't expect Lytle to feel the same way, so there is a generous portion of doubt in my voice when I ask him if he still wants to go on the road trip or back to his mom's house. Before he can answer, my phone rings. It's my sister.

I say, "Hold on a second," and pull into the gas station at the intersection of uncertain destinies.

"Oscar?" Or more like, "Osssss? Currrr? Are you okay? Are you coming? These people won't leave," she pleaded.

"Who? What people?" I ask.

"JJ's back, but they said they won't leave until they get the money I sorta owe them," she responds. "Are you okay?"

"Yes, I'm okay. But really, come if you say you are. I can pay you back after my next show, no problem."

"Now who really are these people?" I ask.

A man's voice ominously says, "Friday afternoon. She owes us."

Then the line is disconnected as I hear what sounds like my sister's voice speaking unintelligibly before getting cut off.

SPOOKY DISTANCE AT AN ACTION

CHAPTER 58

Lytle inquires, "So what's the deal?"

"Uh, my sister again. Some guy sort of threatening . . . She doesn't seem scared but just kind of desperate. I really have to go help her. She wouldn't be playing some bizarre practical joke. I know she's always blamed me or Cigar for her hand and shit, but this is serious. Plus, Nostril Man is on the prowl, and leaving town for a couple of days sounds good. It's just, do you want to go up to NYC still? I totally understand if you don't want to go. Cigar and I will make it fine. I can borrow Carla's truck if you want to stay." I think to myself, It'll only take a couple of hours to go to IBC. I have the keys on me, but I have to call her if I want to borrow it for more than an hour or two. And I know if I talked to her, she would ask me to bring back the camo device.

"What camo device?" asks Lytle. "Dude, you were talking to yourself out loud again."

Was I? Maybe DJ Mike's chemical surprise hasn't entirely worn off. "I told you, man."

"No, you didn't. What camo device?"

"It's what was on the trees at the party."

"Leaves?"

"No, dude, the light show."

"Oh, okay . . . I don't want to stand in the way of you and your light show, so yeah, I'm down . . . I'm totally down. I mean, so far so good as far as I'm concerned. We're only three or four miles from my mom's house, man, and we already managed to shoot a cop's foot off and get a high five from his boss . . . Who knows what we can do in a hundred miles? Not only that, the light show *was* really cool. I'm totally into it. But I thought your rich sister needed thirty-five thousand dollars. What do we do about that? I know, I know, that's kind of why we would go, but . . . Hold on."

"Hold on what?"

"I've got an idea."

THE LION-TRAINER DUDES THAT GOT CREEDLED

"Hey, Cig."

Mr. Cigar crisply stands up on all fours and chirps out a bark.

"Buddy, stay." I reach back in my backpack, retrieving the spray can and remote control. I give Cigar a blast of the video net—or whatever you call it—and switch it to Another One, the camo setting . . . and with the exception of minor distortion around the edges, Mr. Cigar disappears into the back seat of the 2005 Tacoma.

"Holy shit," Lytle squeaks. "That's Carla's invention?"

"Yep. And yep, Cig . . . go get me a Snickers bar, buddy. Lytle: watch."

"Watch what?"

We're parked near the front door of the 7-Eleven with cars on both sides. I crack open the door of the pickup and Cigar squeezes out.

"Oscar . . . Where is he?"

"Check this out, man. Hold on . . . I forgot how this works. Here we go, let's see where he is." I briefly switch the remote from C to L, and Cigar instantly appears on the hood of Lytle's truck, looking at both of us through the windshield.

Startling enough if it was just a dog appearing out of thin air, but for a few seconds on the hood of a pickup truck parked near the front door of a 7-Eleven in Texas is a brightly glowing emerald-green dog that barks once . . . then quickly disappears.

Lytle shrieks like an old lady. I laugh out loud and the guy walking in front of us totally drops his Big Gulp on the sidewalk.

Lytle mutters in quiet amazement, "Lesley Gore Vidal Sassoon! Carla Marks is awwwesome!"

"Yep, and Simon Le Bon Scott Weiland Jennings agrees."

"Nice one, dude," Lytle acknowledges.

"So that's the stuff that was on the trees at the party?"

"Uh-huh . . . and on the DJ."

"Hah!" Lytle exclaims. "Was it on Janis Ian Curtis Mayfield too?"

A few moments later, a dull thump of metal and a slight shifting of light bouncing off the gently flexing hood alert us that Cigar has jumped up on the truck again. Then, to our amazement, two ends of a Snickers bar float in midair. I turn the remote control off, and there's Mr. Cigar on all fours, staring at us with a Snickers bar in his mouth.

"Oh no, oh my God, he did it. I can't believe it. I know Mr. Cigar loves Snickers bars . . ."

For years, every night after dinner me and Cigar would share a Snickers bar with a Diet Pepsi while watching TV. Finally, Mr. Cigar would burp then we could go to bed.

Lytle said in amazement, "Dude . . . he waited for somebody to open the door, snuck in, got a Snickers bar, and did the same thing to get out. He did exactly what you told him, but he knew how to do it. Man, that's insane—he's a human, he's a fucking human man. Ha ha ha, either that or we're dogs."

"I'm fairly sure we're people . . . anyway . . ."

"Yeah, dude."

"I got another idea, Lytle."

"What's that?"

"Let's rob a bank."

OSCAR'S
ELEVEN

"Ah ha ha ha . . . You're serious, right?" Lytle says.

"Yep."

"What are we going to do . . . make Cigar invisible and wait in the getaway car?"

"No, dude."

"No, dude, what?"

"We're not going to make Cigar invisible. We're going to make *you* invisible. I'll wait in the getaway car."

"Whoa, dude. Why don't we, uh, try calling your sister again and see if she hasn't worked this whole thing out? Whatayasay?"

"Ah ha ha. Relax, dude, seriously. I wouldn't make you rob a bank. She's *my* sister, and besides, with Carla's camo unit, there's no way we'll get caught."

"There's always a way, man."

"I know, I know, but check it out. You walk in, take a few—"

"No, *you* walk in."

"Okay, okay. I walk in. I take a few stacks of Benjamins,

and *I* walk out . . . They won't even know they've been robbed. I'll be invisible. It'll be fun. I'll take a little extra and we can buy a couple of bicycles."

"Bicycles?" Lytle queries.

"Yeah, bicycles so we can ride around New York City for a bit, eat some hot dogs, play three-card monte in Central Park. It'll be cool."

"Sounds romantic."

"Don't worry, man. I'm down. I'll do it."

"I mean, how *can* we get caught? Besides, if you use an invisible hand to take something, it's not really stealing, is it? In fact, it's debatable if it ever even happened."

"Definitely."

"It's kinda like taxes."

"Yeah, yeah . . . taxes."

"But we're the government.'

"Yep, we're the government . . . with an invisible hand."

"With an invisible dog that steals Snickers bars."

"Yeah, an invisible tax that Snickers at stealing dogs."

"Ah ha ha ha." Lytle's down, Cigar's down and I'm more than down.

"Okay, then . . . Let's rob a bank."

COUNTING FLOWERS ON THE WALL

With a full tank of gas we ease out of the parking lot north to Interstate 30 toward Little Rock, Memphis and beyond. It's nearing midnight. I'm taking the first driving shift, and Lytle prepares the back seat for his beauty rest while singing a perverted version of a Bob Marley classic. I'm laughing, Cigar is barking and Lytle is singing, "I shot the deputy, but I did not shoot the sher-air-if," literally until he falls asleep.

Barring any more encounters with law enforcement, we should get to Nashville around 9 A.M., rob a bank, maybe shop for a bicycle then grab some breakfast on the way out of town. The sky is clear with a full moon and stars that light up the highway on their own. There is hardly any traffic, and Lytle's mix and the white lines of Interstate 30 provide a mantra for the quick passage of time. As the miles roll by, tomorrow's activities come into focus and a plan is soon hatched. Simple, safe and quick.

WHY DO YOU THINK THEY CALL IT A HOTEL?

CHAPTER 62

We check into a motel short of Nashville, do a practice of sorts, drive into the city and—bam.

Room 132 at the Comfort Inn near Jackson, Tennessee, is the perfect place to practice a bank robbery. The ten-foot walk from the truck to the room is totally chill.

There was no chance management would spot a dog. He's low and quick entering the room, but just in case, I tell Cigar not to bark.

He growls, and I pull out the camo supply, shake the aerosol can and give Lytle a wicked smile. "According to Carla, we have a ton of square footage of camo in this can—if that makes any sense . . . but we got enough to experiment."

"Okay."

"Okay, I'm going to put my wallet over there, and I'm going to make you invisible over here and you're going to go over there and take my wallet."

WHITE SPORT COAT/PINK CRUSTACEAN

Clearly, it's not about skin color, but still, just because a man has clear skin doesn't mean he's a thief . . . He's socioeconomically disadvantaged from growing up in a clear neighborhood.

I'll just stand here and see what it all doesn't look like.

Cigar growls.

I remember Carla's instruction and give Lytle the proper *thwap*. It appears wet when applied to the skin and in a delayed flash it dries or sets up or activates . . . whatever you want to call it . . . like, all at once, everywhere. I turn on the remote control and switch it to camo, and . . . only his head and hands disappear.

"Oh no," Lytle, says, looking in the mirror. "Oh, wow, dude"—he does some weird dance—"this is pretty cool. I look like the invisible man . . . Ah ha ha."

"Yeah, man, but a shirt and a pair of pants would get caught robbing a bank. But . . . wait a second, Lytle. Take off your shirt."

Peeling off his shirt there was an odd-looking moment as it came off his shoulders. But now his torso was way unbelievably transparent. There was another odd moment as I leaned forward to look inside his empty pants.

"That's weird, dude."

"I know, but your pants actually look kind of empty. What does it look like to you . . . in there?"

"It looks weird, dude."

"Ah ha ha."

"Okay, Lytle, I think this is going to work, and yes, it is kind of like the invisible man. So . . . and I thought I'd never say this to my best friend, but . . . take off your pants and steal my wallet. I'm going to watch."

"Freak," Lytle says as his pants and underwear fly across the room . . . hurled by an unseen force.

"That's so cool, man."

"I know . . . That's why I did it."

Cigar growls and tracks Lytle's movement. He apparently can see through the technology. But Lytle is convincingly not there to me. The wallet disappears as a few pieces of it briefly fly into the air—then nothing. Absolutely nothing. It's totally going to work . . .

"Where did you put my wallet?"

"It's under my arm, man."

"Ah ha . . . good idea . . . Don't know why it works, but good idea. Now give me my wallet. Plus, it's creepy that I can't see you . . ."

"Even creepier that I can't be seen." Lytle is talking really close to my ear.

"Ahh, Lytle, you're freaking me out!"

Then without thinking it through I switch the remote to the light show setting, and there before me, closer than expected, is a blindingly green-with-magenta-polka-dots version of Lytle, and I might add that in the brief moment that remote is in light show mode, every detail of Lytle was blindingly green with magenta polka dots? *Every* detail. I instinctively turn it off. Then there before me is actual Lytle—actual *naked* Lytle.

"Duuu—ude!"

"Oh, hold on." I fumble to switch it back to camo mode. Finally . . . invisible.

"Uh . . . here," Lytle says. "Let me put on my clothes."

For yet another unseeable moment a pair of underwear floats up, rotating in midair, assuming the shape of a human waist area . . . this time not so much obscene weirdness but disorienting, ill-defined future weirdness. Something obviously unimaginable that will be considered commonplace sometime soon. Carla Marks . . . I wonder what she'll come up with next.

CRUDITÉS

It's a beautiful day in Nashville. Nine forty-five in the morning, not a cloud in the sky.

Carla says the application would work for about eight hours. Lytle is dead set on doing the deed, so we'll have more than enough time to pull off the heist without reapplying the spray. As we approach City National Bank Branch & Entertainment Office, I pull over and switch Lytle to camo mode. He's taking off his clothes as we pull into the parking lot of 54 Music Square East. It's on Music Row, and I chose it because it had a central location and was in line with the general "music town" vibe.

It doesn't matter what bank we choose because there will be no getaway—so anywhere on Music Row is good, I figure. Cigar and me can walk around like stupid lost tourists, and no one is going to care about the naked invisible black dude. The plan is that we're all gonna walk in to use the ATM, then me and Cig leave while Lytle stays behind to wander around and case the joint. After deciding how to access the teller area, he's going to come outside, tell us how he's going to do it then return for the actual theft, or tax return, or whatever you want to call it. Heck, we'll pay 'em back someday.

Anyway, it won't look weird 'cause we'll walk really slow and I'll be holding a goofy map I bought so me and the dog would look legit.

I say it'll take about fifteen minutes tops. Lytle will come back with money under his arm, whisper in my ear then we'll go back to our car and go see Elvis's house . . .

Oh yeah . . .

That's Memphis.

EL BAILAR

Fully tested for distance and barriers, the camo is in full effect as me, Cigar and Lytle walk through the front door of City National Bank. Just me, a clairvoyant immortal dog and an invisible teenager. That's all. As the door shuts behind us, our odd calmness gives way to a quick chuckle, then a whisper in my ear—"See you on the other side." I can't help chuckling again, and a lady at an ATM looks around. We exchange smiles, and I get a hundred bucks out of my account. Business accomplished.

We return to the beautiful weather. A boy with a dog and a map. Not a cloud in the Nashville sky. Loitering on the sidewalk in front of the bank, sort of looking up in the air and pointing at nothing kind of deal, and seriously, it's way obvious when Lytle comes back to report on the plan. The front door flings open by itself, and I clearly hear his footsteps.

"Dude, it's going to be simple. Two rules. Stay out of people's way and open doors when they aren't looking."

"Sounds like a good plan . . ."

"What's it look like in there?"

"Lots of windows, plenty of room, a hallway with a few meeting rooms then a room full of cubicles and only one door to get to the teller room. You can see inside where the tellers are. There's a big metal rolling thing with stacks of cash on it behind them. It's crazy . . . All I have to do is walk past a few folks then wait until everyone's busy. One, two, three, star on a keypad, then walk in for the old cash-o-reenie."

"Yep."

I stand near the door and watching this lady go in and out a few times. It's easy . . . The windows make it so everyone can see everything—except anything invisible. No doubt some weird '90s security concept. I'm walking back in . . .

"Should take about ten to fifteen minutes. I'll come back out here with twenty grand under each arm, tap you on the shoulder and we'll all walk back to the truck together then go to Graceland."

"That's Memphis."

"I know, I was just making—"

"I got it . . . Be careful . . . Haul ass but take your time."

"Yep."

"I love you, man, Lytle!"

"What?"

"When you come back with the Benjis, we'll make love."

"Ah ha."

Lytle's footsteps disappear toward the bank door.

SEND A SALAMI TO YOUR BOY IN THE ARMY

After a few seconds the door mysteriously flies open, apparently from the wind. Heh heh heh, jeez . . . I should have opened the door for him, but that might have looked sketchy, what with the map and the dog and everything. Much cooler to have the door just magically fly open. Weird, and somehow infinitely easier to explain . . . but Lytle is in the bank . . . undetected.

Then a few minutes later, seemingly out of nowhere, *beep beep beep beep*—an electronic sound my dumb phone has never made. I guess I'm just hoping, but the remote control for the camo system is blinking green, meaning the battery is going dead, which means I have about three minutes before it starts blinking red, which means in thirty seconds a naked teenager will appear in the lobby of a bank or somewhere thereabouts.

Oh, shit. What do I do? Do I just walk into the bank and yell out, "Go back to the truck; the batteries are dying"? I was sort of prepared for this. I have a spare battery. It just never occurred to me that changing the battery while in use would necessitate at least a few seconds of unintended nudity . . . Oh, shit. Then it starts blinking red. Double shit.

Pretty soon, according to Carla, the entire system will go into a blinking mode to warn of the impending blackout—or black-in, per our situation.

THE BATTLE OF THE LOCUSTS

BAM! The front door of the bank flies open, and a second later a security guard comes running out, then for a moment naked Lytle runs maybe thirty feet in front of the rent-a-cop . . . who slows to a brisk jog as he passes me, yelling every time the "naked guy" disappears, "What the fuck?" Naked Lytle reappears for three or four seconds; the guard reorients and repeats, "What the fuck?" Lytle disappears, the guard pauses, says, "What the fuck?" The cycle repeats through the parking lot. It's amazing. The spectacle of the blinking-naked cop chase is so captivating I forget for a second that I should maybe change the battery. It probably takes all of three seconds to get the fresh battery in, power switch on . . . The system takes about that long to boot up, then it flashes once and it's good to go.

I look up and at the end of the parking lot I see the totally dumbfounded mall-cop-lookin' dude oddly chasing an occasionally invisible naked dude who flashes brightly once . . . then—poof. Nothing. Totally bitchin' . . . I can't believe it . . . He made it . . . Ah ha ha . . . I wonder if he got the money.

It all happened so fast. Mr. Cigar was strangely just standing there wagging and gazing toward the action, I guess just acting like a dog.

We begin making our way toward the truck near the end of the parking lot as the wide-eyed Pinkerton dude approaches us, returning to the bank. His mouth is completely agape, repeating, "What the fuck?" into the microphone of a walkie-talkie. As he passes us, staring into the void, I hear a voice on the other end of the transmission going, "Hello Dave? Come in, Dave. Hello? Hello?"

I can't do anything but look down at Cigar to hide my laughter. Poor Dave . . . Sweet guy. He'll know what hit him in a few years.

Seems obvious the best bet is to go back to the truck and wait for Lytle, but before we get there, Cigar barks to announce his arrival, and I hear a breathless, "Hey, dude . . . that was kind of awesome. What the fuck happened?"

"It ran out of juice, man. I don't get it. The battery was fresh; I put it in back at the hotel. I guess it really eats 'em up. I don't remember anything about projected battery life in the manual. Anyway, you're safe, we're cool—plus, it was kind of hilarious. Dude, you should have seen it. It was like . . . a naked guy running, then you would disappear then reappear in a sort of unexpected place. It was like there were a bunch of naked guys just kind of popping on and off in a bunch of different places. It was funny. Like eventually-had-to-look-down-to-change-the-battery funny. Fucking mesmerizing. Were you scared . . . I mean . . . where you were running, man?"

"Dude . . . I was just running. When I realized I was totally invisible again, I stopped. In between all that . . . I was just freaking out. I hadn't really considered the long game up to that point. I'm glad it was funny . . . so glad."

I take a breath. "Dude, I gotta know. You didn't get the money, did you? Heh heh heh."

"No, man. Ha. I was standing near the keypad waiting for this lady who kept going in and out of the tellers' room. Dude, it's so freaky being around people who don't know you're there. You see things.

"Throw in the fact that you know you are naked. IT'S LIKE PHANTOM VISIBILITY. Some profound psychological disruption is bound to occur. It's like the freakin' *Lord of the Rings*, man. Don't wear the ring unless you have to, man . . . You could become its slave. It's twisty, I swear."

"Dude, that's heavy . . . Mr. Invisible Man."

"Anyway, it was weird. I didn't realize I was visible for a while, I guess. But then all of a sudden this fifty-year-old white lady looks at me and screams. I'm kind of used to that, but we never made eye contact, and I hauled ass. By the time I got to the front door, I figured out I was pulsing on and off. Then I started to zigzag for some reason. I guess I was trying to maximize the finite space within which I'd been allowed to operate. It was perfect nick-of-time-type shizzle . . . I was totally at the end of my options and parking lot . . . then that flash . . . It was pretty bright, man, and the security guard kept saying, "What the fuck?" It was sort of funny at that point. Good to be unseen. Apparently, his name was Dave. Man . . . CRACKS ME UP."

"Yeah, man, I heard him too. 'Hello, Dave? Come in, Dave.'"

Much laughter . . . I instinctively head for the highway north. Turn on some tunes, then ask, "So what do we do? Go to Graceland or hit the road?"

"LET'S DO BOTH," Lytle says.

I nod. "I'm hungry, man." As we exit the parking lot, sweet

Dave the security guard (now looking under cars with a flash-light) barely registers our departure. "Put on your clothes, Lytle. Let's go get a taco . . ." I laugh until the British air raid siren screeches from my phone.

SUBVERT THE DOMINANT PARADIGM

"Hello?" Rachel on speakerphone. Not drunk but sort of weird. "Hello, Oscar?"

Really, really, really weird.

"Are you guys coming? These guys are kind of getting impatient. But it's not bad, I mean—"

A man's voice with a vaguely from-somewhere-else accent interrupts, "Hello, Oscar. I hope you are okay. It's just your sister owes me some money, that's all. But everything's okay . . . We are having fun. You are on the road, no? From Texas? I know a great BBQ place in Memphis open twenty-four hours. Anyway. We are having a little party, and we want you to come. Tomorrow at happy hour. Sunset till whenever. On the roof at your sister's place—it's gorgeous. We're here right now. See you, Oscar? Can we count on you?"

With a fake-jovial laugh, he says, "YOU MUST COME!"

I don't know what to say.

"Bye-bye, Oscar. It's thirty-five thousand. I know, I know . . . fake pleading . . . but it's for your seester . . . It's for your seester . . . Oscar, I know you are coming. Take care. Bye-bye . . ." *Click.*

WHAT HAS GONE WRONG iS STiLL GOING WRONG

Cigar barks. Lytle, now clothed, has that *what the hell just happened, we gotta go, get out of my way* look on his face . . . so I assume he's all gung ho and shit. It's about fifteen hours from Nashville to New York City . . . It's noon now. We got just enough time to rob a bank, get to the Big Apple, and even catch a few hours' sleep before the big party. That guy did sound sort of creepy, and it does sound like she's *kind of* being kidnapped. But all he wants is money. I know about her ex . . . It's that simple.

"Lytle, buddy . . . I actually can't wait to rob a bank. Naked. Invisible and rich. Sounds like a groovy thing to me."

"Yeah, but we'll only be rich for a couple of hours."

"Well, you know what they say. It's better to have loved and lost . . ."

"Than never to have gone totally undefeated?"

I blow him a kiss. "That's so romantic."

THE INDIAN IN
THE TOOLBOX

Highway 81 is the longest odd-numbered interstate highway in which the number does not end with a five . . . It traces the paths created down the length of the Appalachian Mountains by migrating animals, American Indians and early settlers. Once a major corridor for troop movement during the great Civil War is now used for human trafficking and the War on Drugs. For clarification purposes, I capitalize "War on Drugs," but I am not referring to the war Richard M. Nixon declared back in the '70s, a war that ended in dismal defeat for the US. No, I am not speaking of a war *against* drugs. I'm talking about a war high *on* drugs. Now however, on this very day, I-81 is more a byway for magical dogs, bank robbers and teenage geniuses with a plan than for any other kind of war. Whether high or not!

The plan is to get to New York City with thirty-five grand by sunset tomorrow.

Truly genius in its simplicity. However truly lacking in substance.

But who needs substance when you are going invisible,

naked and willing to put your foot on the gas until you get to where you think you wanna go? We take 40 out of Nashville to hook up with 81 outside of Knoxville. Google says there's a couple of banks close to the highway in the downtown area of Knoxville. Good enough for me.

We stop at a Starbucks, as one does. Lytle waits in line, and I go to the restroom, take off my clothes and get invisible. It's like a physical rush. Super weird. Like vertigo. No one notices as a slightly obscured bundle of clothes floats out the back door of a Starbucks and makes its way to Lytle's truck.

Cigar barks a hello as I hop into the back. Lytle returns with what he calls a sugar coffee, and we make our way to the Bank of America on Main Street, just a few blocks away. I'm naked and invisible, and the wireless controller has a fresh battery.

I figure I have at least forty-five minutes.

And, man . . . Lytle was right: there is a certain state of mind that one reaches by experiencing self-invisibility. It's not necessarily an all-powerful, beyond-all-other type of sensation. But more of a *holy shit . . . they can't see me, and I'm naked* deal. It brings an instant smile to your face—a smile of wonder, and friendly wonder at that. It really doesn't feel negative in any kind of way.

TWENTY-MULE TEAM BORAX

Despite the evil that could be perpetrated with such a device, I feel oddly confident that I'm doing no wrong. But most certain, despite the overriding bank-robbery thing, deception (clinical deception) is at the core of this power. And deception as a concept just doesn't feel like the golden ticket to heaven. Elation and regret in an emotional sense, logical in the real, but I'm leaning toward Lytle's *Lord of the Rings* theory. It's devilishly delicious.

Carla must truly be from outer space. I mean, really, the woman who fell to earth or something. First the water sheet and now the video net. She's on a roll and has been telling me for the past year or so that she's working on another subatomic machine system . . . but this project she said had more of an analog feel. More organic. Imagine a lens that could be almost an infinite number of discrete focal lengths at any particular moment. Faster than you can think it . . . times a googol . . . or two. Then a generation faster even than that. In a spray-paint can at pico scale

"I want my car to go a generation faster."

"No, Oscar . . . Indeed you don't."

I love Carla.

For some reason, I remember eating fried pies with my father. When at our lake house we would drive up into the Arbuckle Mountains and eat lunch at the same place, outside of who-knows-where, for dessert my dad always had a fried peach pie and I had chocolate . . . and peach.

TiC-TAC-
PTOMAiNE

Lytle parks in a lot next to the Bank of America. I'm naked and motivated. As good a time as any to rob a bank.

Crossing Locust Street to the front entrance, I notice cars don't slow down too much for invisible people. I walk in the front door, not caring at all about doors just flying open, and negotiate my way to the money room. Having to wander just a bit was something I had anticipated. For some reason, floor plans for Bank of Americas are mysteriously unavailable online. Especially for the downtown Knoxville, Tennessee, branch. Anyway, the going was powerfully good. I couldn't resist blowing on a stack of papers in front of a copy boy standing at a printing kiosk in the middle of a room full of cubicles.

Making my way to the center of the hive, I find the most obvious candidate for the door that leads to the queen and a handful of her royal jelly. You can hear lots of buzzing around it, and it is actually propped open about 8 inches. You can see right through to the tellers seated. A guard is walking around the opposite side of a metal rolling cart, preparing to wheel it out of the room.

Holy shit, this is a no-brainer. I can make it through that space in like seconds. I glance down to get cursory assurance as to my invisibility then slip easily inside the pit of cash in front of the cart and guard. The door barely moves. The guard is either taking something away or has just delivered something in the cart. My guess is the "something" is cash, but either way I can see the only supply of stacked hundreds is sitting in the tellers' drawers who in turn were sitting in rolling swivel chairs, belly-up to the trays of dough.

I need thirty-five thousand–ish for the mission, and I can plainly see there is easily that much in bundled hundreds. The problem there is, no one teller has that much in their drawer. I will have to get it from two drawers. So I might as well grab $40,000. No difference to me.

I'm comfortable, I'm clearly invisible and for once I give thanks to Kenny G, whose soothing licks, pumped into the bank's overhead speakers, mask the sound of escalating breathing and any crinkling my feet might make on the impossible-to-describe-colored carpet. I've been invisible for about ten minutes. I do have a good fifteen left in my self-imposed limit of twenty-five. However, my battery, like everybody's, eventually will die, and I really want to avoid another Nashville Lytle shuffle.

Pretty soon, I've got to make a move.

YAHOO MOUNTAIN DEW

"Wahoo" is the word. As a noun, it could be a Scombridae fish found worldwide in tropical/subtropical seas, or a shrubby spindle tree from eastern North America also called "burning bush." As a verb, a southern United States (meaning Texas, and by Texas I mean Texas and Oklahoma combined) term for a variation of the classic smash-and-grab burglary technique, an in-your-face style of robbery that is characterized by a surprise-then-take-it-by-any-means-but-leave-a-tip mentality. Closely compares as well to the time-honored bum-rush, an overwhelming strategy characterized again by surprise, relying then on outnumbering security (whatever that might be).

Also, when used in a sentence, it doesn't describe an actual technique but more correctly a lack of technique. The plan is that there *is* no plan. You do what makes sense in the moment, and generally speaking any planning is done during the crime itself or in the few moments leading up to the actual commission. The most common things to wahoo are smaller items that when purchased are under some kind of restriction either by age of customer, the hour of need, the actual penal code or any combination thereof.

Wahooing doesn't rely so much on flashy violent gestures, threats or numbskull brutality. It's more of an artistic sort of endeavor or perhaps even a dance. This gives it a spiritual characteristic that further separates it from most other similar endeavors. Often with a comical theme, it's a true southern tradition, but if ever you expect to have any sort of longevity in your career as a wahoo dancer, do it maybe once or twice in your entire life, use only as a last option and make sure you tip the ride operator . . . on the way out.

So things like beer and cigarettes are commonly wahooed.

Example: A seventeen-year-old walks into an appropriate convenience store after legal beer-buying hours. As he walks to the cooler section, an accomplice enters the store, slightly stumbling to the lone cashier. The accomplice clutches his stomach, and his white T-shirt stands in stark contrast to the fake blood in his midsection—the clutched area. He mumbles, "I, I've been . . ." while looking directly into the eyes of the person behind the counter. The first guy in the store now has a couple of twelve packs of Miller Lite in his hands and is making his way back to the front door. He jogs outside while a third accomplice holds the door open, partially blocking the "beer man's" escape route. The horrified cashier can't take his eyes off the apparent stabbing victim when suddenly the bloody accomplice completes his belabored sentence—"I've been . . . I, I've been dishonest with you"—and as he straightens up . . . the hands once clutching his midsection suddenly reveal a couple of twenties, which are tossed on the counter as the bloody fake victim sprints out the front door laughing. The stunned clerk takes the forty bucks, sticks it in his pocket and typically never calls the police. The fake blood was Big

Red soda that "stabbed guy" happened to spill on himself in the car on the way over. Beer-less to beer-full in just shy of twenty seconds.

Classic time-studied perfection. No plan, unintentionally synchronized comedic action and victory. A sacred obligation realized with a mutual flow of consideration: the dude got money, the party got beer, everybody laughed . . . the funny trifecta.

As far as the here and now is concerned, I'm following my own recommendations. Aside from actually being the fake-bloody guy in the story, it feels like I have no other good option. I'm naked and invisible (that's the comedy part), and my plan consists of ending up in the truck safely with thirty-five thousand under my arms. The no-plan plan is in full effect. In this case I won't be able to tip the ride operator on the way out. So it looks like I'm just gonna have to go in and wahoo it without the tip.

COLD NiGHT FOR ALLiGATORS

Standing in the middle of tellers two and three, I grab the inside of their back supports and rotate both forward and inside about thirty degrees. I pause for a moment then firmly (as hard as I can) pull both straight back while screaming at the top of my lungs. The tellers tumble harmlessly out of their chairs, more out of incredulity than out of angular acceleration. Then, relying more on theater as opposed to physical violence, I grab handfuls of dollar bills, whirl around, facing the gaping audience then throw both fistfuls into the air above them.

Just for good measure, I give one more bloodcurdling scream, making sure they can all hear and see where it came from. All four tellers get a huge, wide eyeful of dimly lit flying teeth and wildly gesticulating tongue, a view of the action. They totally lose it and fall back to the wall. Stepping toward the cash, I grab four stacks of hundreds. Then, pivoting toward the exit, I'm gone . . . before the last thrown bills settle to the ground. I jog carefully around the scattered bodies, flinging the door wildly open, scooting out,

GiBBY HAYNES

Kenny G still wafting through the workplace as a woman's voice breaks the drone with a horrifying disgusted southern drawl, mournfully lamenting, "You could see its *may-outh*," followed then by a deeply soul-questioning male voice: "My *Lo-werd*."

LASER TAG

I can't help but laugh out loud while making my way through the cubicle room. Tossing a trash can in the opposite direction and heading to the front door, I hear the same woman's wildly pathetic moan-scream. A simple but desperately desperate "I don't *nay-oh*" adds little hope to an obviously collapsing belief system . . . floating off into the great unheard.

Out the front door, turning the corner, I'm gone.

Lytle and Mr. Cigar come into focus, sprinting across Locust Street to the parking lot . . . I'm there.

"Check it out, man." I reveal armpits full of Franklins. "It was crazy . . . I had to show my teeth! Duuude, it made the Circle K Big Red wahoo look junior high."

"That *was* junior high, dude."

"Yeah . . . but forty-K junior high."

"Ahhhhhh . . . I seeeee."

"Check it out, L . . ."

Smelling a stack of hundreds, thumbing it like a deck of cards, Lytle chuckles.

"Lytle, I'm thinking maybe you should go back into the

bank and get some money from the ATM so we don't look like . . . bank robbers bookin' with the spray. I'll just stay invisible in the truck while you go. Cool?"

"No." Lytle shakes his head. "I'll pretend you didn't say 'bookin' with the spray.' Other than that, yes, and I'll be back in a second. Stay, Cig!"

An alarm from the bank erupts from the other side of Locust Street.

"Whoa, dude!"

"No, no, no, it's cool . . . Lytle, just pretend you're . . . whatever . . . Just try to walk into the bank and get some gas money or whatever."

"Okay, man."

WIDE SCHMOOTH OPEN

Lytle disappears around the corner and comes back a little too soon for a cash withdrawal. As he rounds the corner, he's wide-eyed at the windshield. Not actually focusing on me, and from what I can tell . . . laughing his ass off.

Approaching and laughing through the open window.

"You won't believe it, man . . . Where are you? Are you in the back . . . Ah ha ha, I can see your ass outline movin' around on the seat. Anyway, they wouldn't let me in the building. The security guard was at the door sayin', 'I'm sorry, sir, the bank is closed.' Then this lady comes out the door behind him with a trash can over her . . . spooky-head . . . It was really muffled, but it sounded like she was talking or shrieking or crying about '*Heez may-outh*' over and over. Freaky, dude. Totally . . . abstract."

I nod.

"What did you do to those poor people in there?"

"I made an omelet, man!"

"How many eggs did you have to break?"

"Oh, dude . . . It was definitely a three-egg omelet . . . with chili and cheese."

"Ah ha ha ha!"

"But I did get forty grand."

Sweet.

We can definitely afford my sister's "party," AND a couple of bikes with a basket for Mr. Cigar to ride around in—

Bark!

"That's groovy, man, but we need to ease outta here before you get visibly naked, dude. I've been there, and it's a gnarly row to hoe."

"Row to hoe?"

"Yes, row to hoe."

"What does that even mean?"

"My family's in the gardening business . . . You wouldn't understand."

"Sure you don't mean a hoe to row?"

"I'm sure I don't want a hoe to row."

"Enough!" I mumble. But pulling out of the lot onto Main, heading toward 81 and the "big party," I have to stop and marvel at our accomplishments. "Wow, man . . . We did it."

"Yep, we totally robbed a bank."

"Now I guess we ought to head for the Big Apple? We only have a little over twenty-four hours and it's a ten- to twelve-hour drive."

"I know . . . I also know I'm hungry."

"Cool, man. Let's get a taco."

FLAT AS A KANSAS CORNFLAKE

Dinner is less than awesome. I take the first truck shift while Lytle DJs and makes up bad jokes. Cigar growls at the conclusion of every awful pun, and both him and Lytle finally pass out while I continue driving. I believe the straw that broke the comedian's back was Lytle's oft-repeated "What kind of bird's bottom-end helps you see better?" joke. The punch line being "gull asses," then the inevitable "Get it? . . . Gu-lasses." Mr. Cigar doesn't even growl at that point . . . He just rolls over and starts snoring. Lytle soon follows.

I'm still way amped from the Knoxville job earlier. Wide awake coming up on the Pennsylvania border. It's midnight, and just as we're crossing the Mason-Dixon line my phone rings . . .

It's Miss Carla Marks.

Plus, I've only been answering the phone when it's my sister, and Carla has called like five times, maybe six. I mean, we've been robbing banks and shit for the past few days, and I just haven't had much time to talk. What with drug-running and shot-up police officers and all. Plus the romance of the highway.

Cigar barks, and Lytle says, "What are you talking about, man?"

"Oh, sorry, dude . . . I was just talking to myself. It's Carla—she's tried calling me maybe a billion times."

"Looks like she's up late."

DIXIE CUPS

The Mason-Dixon line is one of those things you study in a class that's so boring you refuse to dignify its existence and permanently erase it from all forms (present and future) of internal data storage. That means it was probably a Texas history course. I would know for sure, but I intentionally forgot. It's not that Texas history isn't the greatest story ever told. I mean, I really love Davy Crockett bowie knives and even one-legged Mexican generals in drag, not to mention rancid shark oil, cannibals and big, big, big petrochemical . . . but by the time I was in seventh grade I had taken Texas history four or five times. I might even have taken it twice in sixth grade. It's difficult to say . . . I know I totally erased at least one of 'em, and the rest just sort of blend in and out of each other.

Anyway, the Mason-Dixon has some revolutionary war significance; however, in the latter part of the nineteenth century it became the dividing line between the north and the south, everything southern being the land of Dixie (Dixon—get it?). My preference is to refer to it as the "y'all line" . . . to the north of the Mason-Dixon it's "you guys." The farther south you go, the y'all-er it gets.

HiGH SCHOOL REUNiON

"Carla, what's going on?"

"I'm glad I was able to reach you, Oscar. Sorry to call so late, but I was a bit worried, really. I noticed you haven't been staying in my guesthouse the past couple of nights but the company truck has and was concerned as to your welfare. Especially in light of the Colonel Sanders disaster-thon who has by the way left town . . . I think. So, anyway, how are you?"

"I'm good. I mean, *we're* good. I'm with Lytle."

"That's nice—say hello. How is Lytle?"

"He's good."

"What's going on . . . Are you guys camping out or something?"

"No, we're not camping out. Actually, Nostril Man was on the rampage and staked out both your house and my parents'. We crashed out at Lytle's mom's then hit the road."

"That was my suspicion, Oscar. The good colonel was super aggressive after you escaped out the back . . . He was singularly focused on Mr. Cigar. I feared he had tracked you down somehow, so I'm relieved to find you're okay . . . You're on the road you say? Where are you?"

"Well, it's a long story, Carla, but we decided to go to New York for a few days and stay at Rachel's."

"Oh . . . That sounds about right. How nice. Say hello to Rachel . . . Her new painting looks great in the dining room. Tell her she's incredible."

"I'll be sure to, Carla. We should get to the city in the morning . . . maybe around noon."

"Oh, goodness, you're not there yet? Where are you?"

"We're on Highway 81, just crossed over the Mason-Dixon."

"Ah ha, be careful! Are you actually driving?"

"Yeah."

"Oh . . . I'll let you drive. Say hello to Cigar as well, and I assume you have the video net unit with you? We haven't really talked about that since the party."

"Oh yeah, Carla. I'm sorry. Nostril Man scared the crap out of me, and I ran out of the trailer with it in my hands . . . It's been in my backpack ever since."

"Okay, Oscar. I trust you to take care . . . It's one of the only prototypes, of which one is loaned out to the US military, and as you might imagine, it's fairly hush-hush now, so don't go showing it to any North Korean spies. When are you guys coming back?"

"Oh yeah, Carla. We're cool . . . as long as Nostril Man isn't a total troll when we get back to Perfectville."

"No, Oscar, I believe he's gone for the time being. We'll talk about that when you get back. Hopefully three or four days? Be careful, though . . . and have fun at your sister's."

"Cool, Carla. My sister is having a party tomorrow night, and that's kind of the reason we're going. We'll probably ride bikes and crash out in Central Park tomorrow afternoon, go to the party . . . stay at Rachel's for two or three nights then head back."

"Sounds lovely, Oscar. Please answer when I call . . . I'm concerned."

"Don't worry, Carla . . . Our 'crazy' is eating at Cracker Barrel . . . We're good."

"Well, do say hello to Rachel, don't give Cigar any ice cream and call me when you settle in. Be careful, Oscar. Talk to you soon."

"Okay, Carla . . . Love you."

"Love you too, Oscar. Are you sure you guys are all right?"

I hang up without answering and glance behind me, as Lytle is already back to sleep. Cigar is standing on the platform, staring at me, wagging away.

Energized, I continue north on 81 passing Harpers Ferry. We change drivers in Harrisburg, head east on 78, an early morning breakfast (Waffle House), then through the Holland Tunnel . . . landing in Manhattan just shy of 10 A.M.

With seven hours until party time and five grand more than we think we need, Lytle, me and Mr. Cigar decide to make good on my promise and head to the nearest bicycle shop.

DENATURED ALCOHOL

I opt for the ageless beach-cruiser style, but instead of the classic Schwinn, I get the titanium version. It weighs in at nineteen pounds, four of which are seat, and you can pop a sustained mellow wheelie effortlessly for like a block. Lytle got a perfectly restored—or new-old stock or something—orange Krate Stingray from the '70s. Tiny front wheel, sissy bar, ape hangers, and that crazy springer front end. It also has stupid pneumatic shocks and a stick shift.

For my head protection, I get the low-key flat black skate-board style but Lytle goes to the sporting goods place next door and gets a football helmet. They made the wrong size for some kid so Lytle gets it totally cheap. He has 'em take the face mask off. The helmet itself is metal-flake gold with a black racing stripe, and it says WILDCATS on both sides. A stunning stroke of brainlessness but awesomely cool . . .

I think both bikes come in around five grand but I get a little crazy and add in the "totally British" wicker basket for Mr. Cigar. It's really cool . . . all leather and bamboo with a brass badge on the front where you can put whatever, and for an extra twenty they had a machine that would engrave it. I went for the full monty. They wrote GANGSTA on it in Edwardian script and mounted the whole thing on my front handlebars.

VOLCANIC ISLAND PARADISE

We roll out of the store, put the bikes in the truck and park in a garage on West Fifty-Fifth Street. It costs like $75 an hour but, hey, you only go around once—plus, we're rich, naked and invisible (when we want to be). Maybe it isn't reality, but today at Columbus Circle, crossing Central Park South on Broadway, it feels more like real fun than not. Me on a titanium cruiser, Mr. Cigar jumping up and down in his wicker chariot, Lytle on the wayback machine, crazily shifting gears, blowing out huge vape hits, wearing a metal-flake gold football helmet. I feel like I'm still tripping . . . so high.

Up the west side of Central Park . . . past Strawberry Fields, all the way to the Jackie O Reservoir. Make a giant loop east, coming down to the Metropolitan Museum of Art. The feeling of doing/seeing something for the first time is energizing. Even though you know you'll never do this thing again, it never really crosses your mind, so the moment seems pure. Who cares? "Doing it again" is overrated anyway. Nonetheless, the drive from the Knoxville wahoo is catching up with me/us. So we find an awesome spot on the grass and sit down next to our bikes and Mr. Cigar. We're on a mellow hillside with a view of the museum. The grass is cool to the touch. We eat two hot dogs each (six total) and now, thankfully, take a little nap. Before we totally crash, I agree with Lytle and Mr. Cigar that it would be best to arrive fashionably late for the big party at Rachel's. I mean, I have no way of getting ahold of her other than walking right up to her front door, so I guess we'll be fashionable. With thirty-five grand in our pockets I'm not worried. After all, we do have Mr. Cigar. Not only that . . . it's an awesome day. Cool enough for the sun to feel great. There's a brilliant blue, newly washed sky where almost every occasional cloud looks like a blank-staring teddy bear and, not to mention . . . this grass feels grrreat. This is going to be nice.

I set my alarm for 5 P.M. and pass out.

THE STAR OF A HOLLYWOOD MOVIE

I dream that I'm underneath a basketball goal attached above the driveway opening to a typical suburban garage. Somebody is by my side. We somehow have a clear 360-degree view of the impossibly obstructed horizon. Alone now and surrounded by a maze of two-story garage apartments, I can actually feel the approaching monsters . . . like fourth-grade math class—horrible—then suddenly over the apartment roof at the end of my endless driveway appears a giant curved-tusked flying elephant whose gaze would strike you dead . . . and behind him a trained tornado. As fear-inducing as the giant flying Medusa elephant is, the trained tornado has no rival in its ability to project fear of imminent death . . . paralyzing. Then suddenly the sky turns into cookies made with a dough containing the ashes of all things I've ever written on paper. I keep them in a box for nine years then feed them to people in the parking lot at an NFL football game. Somehow I become fabulously wealthy . . . I feel horrible . . . then I wake up. Nice one, Oscar. Me and Lytle play our dream-telling game.

Lytle says, "I dreamed that I was a dog named Fulcrum, coughing up grass eaten in a field made of Shellfish known as Flake-Berry Village, where vibrating rain-soaked tourists stuttered odd commands at a chalk-white, six-foot-tall penis they called Harrison Ford. Awkwardly, my water grass vomit rolled backward into a cave that was somehow under the beach while we waited for dumb, bodiless pirates to steal our boogers and laugh at the clock made of silent diamonds. They never came, and the clock wasted all of its time licking rich girls right between their eyes. Then I woke up."

"That was pretty nuts."

"Yeah."

"Wow, dude, you pretty much smoked mine . . .

"It was close."

"Especially the backward-rolling grass vomit. The absolute kiss of victory in the business of dreams."

"Oh, absolutely."

"Remember the first fake-dream contest ever?"

"They're real dreams!"

"Okay . . . It's just a term . . . They're not really fake."

"Good."

"All right . . . You sucked at first, dude. I totally smoked you every time until you did that two-minutes-of-silence thing and when I interrupted—seriously . . . I remember this shit—I said, 'Okay, I get it, you dreamed of nothing . . . awesome . . .'"

"No . . ."

"Remember . . . then I said, 'So . . . of what did you dream? Then you went blank . . . and this was my favorite part because of that look . . . Dude, you totally sold me . . . It was awesome, and you said it was too intense to describe, man. Do you remember that? Still cracks me up."

"Totally, dude . . . like it was yesterday. I didn't say it was too intense, though. I said 'impossible.' It was impossible to describe. There was/is really no way to express it. Even if it was intense, I would have been oblivious to it . . . I experienced the impossible in an almost pure form, however just possible enough to activate an attempted internal comparison . . . dig?"

"Wow."

"Yeah, man . . . It's been like two years of dreams. We should write a book . . . of dreams."

"Yep."

"Dreams are, like, totally real, Pepsi Man."

"Wow, Lytle, can I quote you on that? And did you call me Pepsi Man?"

"Sure."

"Can I put it on a poster with a kitten hanging from a clothesline?"

"Yep . . . What time is it, dude? We slept a while."

CASPER THE FRIENDLY GHOST

It is four-thirty. The phone rings . . . It's Rachel's number. Three rings, "Hello" . . . then the same male voice as before, with a vague from-somewhere-else accent.

"Hello, Oscar."

"Hey, hey."

"This is Ricky, Rachel's friend. How are you? I'm calling to make sure you're okay . . . I hope you made it to the city, man."

"Yeah, yeah, we're here."

"Great to hear, great to hear, Oscar. So . . . you are coming to our party, no? Of course you are."

"It's what, four-thirty now?"

"Be here when you get here, man . . . It's all good. Just come in the front door. The code is pound-two-two-four-four. Come to the elevator and press R . . . We'll be having a proper good time. That's pound, two, two . . . four, four. It's gonna be a blast."

"Yep."

"Here's Rachel."

"Hey, buddy."

"Hey, Rachel."

"I'm so glad you made it, Oscar. Thank you so much . . . Don't worry, these guys are basically sweeties. Ricky likes to act like a gangster, but he's really a teddy bear. And I *do* feel really bad for you guys to come all the way up to New York from home . . . in a truck. Hope you don't mind me calling you first. I really need this, sweetie . . . I would have called Mom, except I talk to her like only on holidays, but whatever, I'm glad you're here. And you're my bro!"

"It's okay, Rachel. I owe you . . . Besides that, you're my sister. Guess we'll see you in an hour or so. Think it's okay if we crash at your place?"

"Yeah, totally cool. We'll do something groovy tomorrow."

"Sounds good, Rach. See you in a bit."

"Bye, Oscar."

A PLEASANT SURPRISE iS STiLL A SURPRISE

Wow, that's the friendliest, sort of upbeat Rachel I've heard in a while. Kind of nice. Oddly. Sure doesn't sound like she's almost being kidnapped. Our last forty-eight hours have been crazy even by crazy standards. Now I'm starting to think the big finale is going to be kind of a letdown. I mean, anything compared to dope dealin', amputation and grand larceny is going to look mellow, but this feels as if it might actually be fun. People and music and stuff like that fun. You never know. A pleasant surprise is pleasant . . . nonetheless still surprising.

Walking our bikes up the hill toward the jogging path, we go through a tree tunnel of what appear to be giant oaks. Immune, I think, to their sound (like living near a train track), I pause and accidentally listen to this huge green room, tap Lytle on the shoulder and point upward. He says, "What, dude?" then looks up.

"Listen."

"Oh yeah, man, I didn't notice 'em either. Funny."

MOUTH FROM THE SOUTH

They're actually loud as shit. Didn't know they had cicadas in Central Park. Referring to Brood X of the magicicada periodical cicada, of course . . . apparently alive and well in New York City . . . and indeed ready to party for their big and only summer. For seventeen years, these babies have been underground. Hands down my favorite insect. Big Texas male appeal. Large and loud. Can't say enough! You tie a four-foot length of thread around their little insect necks, toss 'em in the air and they skitter around like airborne trout. Or, sadly, they will instinctively grab onto a firecracker. So you hand them a black cat, light the fuse and let 'em go. They fly surprisingly well despite the added weight . . . for like three seconds. Then things get elliptical. Not exactly in line with the teachings of the Buddha. But less cruel, methinks, than the Oscar-style fate of another childhood bug . . . The firefly. Or in Texan, lightning bug. What one does is: mash their little glow-in-the-dark butts in a circular motion on the underside of a Frisbee . . . then enjoy a poetically demented light show while tossing a flying disc on a beautiful summer evening. Or you can just smush one directly across your sister's forehead on a beautiful summer evening . . . when you're eleven years old and it's her birthday.

And there's the roly-poly, aka the pill bug. In my neighborhood, it's a roly-poly. A favorite insect for me because they're not really an insect. They're a terrestrial crustacean . . . commonly found on decaying corpses. Darkly FYI. When stressed, they roll up into tiny black armored balls. For sport? You agitate them into the ball state and flick them around with leaf stems like you're playing a miniature game of hockey. The goals are the little sand pits the antlion makes. Antlions rock. Their nomenclature bears no geographic assertion. There are antlions everywhere, I presume. (Given the fantasy they conjure as lion-sized ants, Texans are likely to believe antlions came from "up north" and began terrorizing the south soon after the war.) Ant-sized lions are just as scary but way more funny. A 250-pound ant is one thing, but lions one-sixteenth of an inch long . . . Really takes the fun out of the old stomping-on-a-giant-nest thing. Plus, you need a handful and a quiet moment to hear 'em roar.

In human scale: You are walking along, minding your own business, and tumble into a thirty-foot sand pit . . . Every time you crawl to the top, just as escape seems possible, you are hit by sixty pounds of well-delivered rocks. You fall back to the bottom, and this process continues until you are exhausted, badly beaten, lying at the bottom of the pit. Then a giant pair of scissors cuts you in half. That's the basic antlion experience . . . in human scale. That's only the larval phase of this creature. The innocent child of the species. Logically, then, the adults of the species should become evil brain-eating skin peelers. But no. This wicked child-sect becomes a slender, sort of elegant, flying creature. Think dragonfly. Maybe Lytle and

I are just a couple of crazy bugs trying to cope with those "difficult larvae" years, and we will become elegant flying creatures . . . Someday. It definitely feels like we're becoming something. Whatever . . . feels great?

HORIZON ZERO

Out the south end of Central Park, we head back to the parking garage. We cross Central Park South, once again a beautiful event. The titanium-stingray metal-flake happy-dog . . . alone in the tube . . . totally shacked!

Downtown toward Fifty-Fifth, we pass Carnegie Hall.

"The birthplace of intelligent dance music," offers Lytle. Hee-larious.

Parking costs like $3,846. Oh well . . . This *is* New York City, after all.

Back in the truck on the mean streets of the Big Apple . . . tourists, cops, people in suits and a guy with a Barbie doll woven into his hair. We stop in search of Dr Pepper and a bag of Fritos. No such luck. The dude behind the counter points down the block, and in a heavy Indian accent says, "We do not have this 'Fritos,' but you might try the new deli across the street." Lytle cracks up . . . I chuckle, and the guy behind the counter laughs harder than both of us. A few minutes later, we're in Times Square. Visually visual. A splash of neon, stand-still traffic, horns honking and hordes of people horde-ing the sidewalk. For a New York neophyte, just approaching Times Square at rush hour is like whitewater rafting a turbulent section of the Snake River in the spring. The canyon walls of Manhattan, both nauseating and claustrophobic, rise sharply from either side, then at Forty-Seventh Street disintegrate into the gut feeling of going to the basement in a really fast elevator . . . dramatically revealing an overwhelming landscape of dancing lights, naked cowboys and Statues of Liberty.

"Ah, Little Tokyo," Lytle muses. "There must be a billion lights."

"At least, man. And for every light on Broadway . . . a broken heart."

I laugh, then we're both laughing . . . at things that are there and really shouldn't be. *And* things that should be but actually aren't. Times Square is a jarring experience, even unadulterated. Additionally, a not-so-vague trail of lights (with any movement of my eyes) makes things extra fresh, if not slightly entertaining. Testimony, undoubtedly, to my recent experience. I swear; DJ Mike must have given me a tablespoon of that shit. Almost three days later, I still feel like I'm tripping. But maybe Times Square always feels like an electric box of crayons from which there is no exit. You don't really leave. You escape. We manage the escape . . . unscathed.

But I can't help feel like I'm not out of danger. There is something going on . . . like an extra layer . . .

Layer of what, though? Secret fucking sauce?

Encroaching destiny?

It's hard to tell. I have no frame of reference. I hate McDonald's . . . for political reasons.

A series of perfectly staggered green lights plunges us into an obstacle course of buses and taxis.

Then traffic thins out a bit. The windows are open, and Mr. Cigar noses the breeze downtown to Rachel's apartment.

This is my first time driving an automobile in New York City. I've taken a few cab rides, but, despite what one hears, driving is way easier than expected. Surprisingly not as bad as North Dallas at rush hour. Twenty degrees cooler, same angry drivers and actually fewer cars. Rachel's apartment is in the SoHo section of town. We get to her street, and it's a short five blocks to the crib. SoHo is a funny part of the city for the first-timer. You'd think it would be the Theater District, like the Soho area of London, but no, that's Broadway here. SoHo, in NYC, is a combo name that stands for "south of Houston." Meaning south of Houston Street. Extra odd if one is a first-timer from Texas. To a Texan . . . Galveston is south of Houston, not a part of New York City. Odder even, up here it's pronounced HOW-stun not HUGH-stun. Don't ask why. Nobody knows, and they'll probably mention that it's like the way they pronounce "Rodeo" in Los Angeles. Which is "row-DAY-owe." Sacrilege to any true Texan. Rachel's street is similar to a lot of streets in the city. A bunch of ratty (literally) redbrick buildings with garbage flying around, homeless people and drug addicts. It's a nice area. The crappy neighborhoods are basically the same but instead of garbage flying around it's bullets. Like an American high school . . .

Lytle pulls into another parking garage—easy but expensive. We walk the half block to my sister's, punch in the access code. Seconds later, we're on our way up.

I'm trying to call Rachel, but there's no service in this ancient elevator, and it rises about an inch a minute. Not only that but it's carpeted, making for a claustrophobic cotton-in-your-ears type of experience. If nothing else, the tension is rising as Lytle, me and Mr. Cigar stand side by side staring straight ahead, our gaze only slightly angled upward. Typical elevator posture . . . but on high alert. A bell anounces the arrival to each successive floor.

Finally, Lytle, right around bell number ten, chops the moment in half and says to no one in particular, "Buddy Rich Little Stevie Ray Charles Manson Family Affairs of the Heart of Darkness at the Edge of Townes Van Zandt."

All I could manage in response was, "Wow."

The elevator doors open into a small box-shaped room. I can hear music through the walls. Cigar's ears stiffen. I glance at Lytle. He pushes through the room's metal door, revealing a huge tiled rooftop, with potted plants, tables, chairs and couches arranged in various hangout areas. There's even a little kitchenette with a grill and refrigerator. Kind of sweet.

But there's no bartender. No party people. No snacks.

SPOCK,
HELP ME

The door behind us makes a resounding slam shut.

Cigar starts barking. Lytle winces. I pause for a moment, surveying the layout. I round the corner to see the rest of the roof . . . There's Rachel, looking a little older and stressed, sitting on the couch beside a Euro-looking dude I've never seen before. But that's no big deal . . . I don't know what a lot of her friends look like . . . actually, none of 'em.

The Euro-dude is looking at us with wide eyes in obvious (but weird) anticipation. He taps his iPhone, and the music fades.

"Hello, Oscar! You must be Lytle. And, of course, Mr. Cigar . . .

"We're having a little party."

Cigar keeps barking, acting super jumpy. Lytle slumps a little in the realization that this isn't the party I know he was looking forward to. But I don't mind . . .

I knew it wasn't going to be a giant blowout. Certainly not an "Oscar and the clown" party. I'm actually relieved. We'll do this money thing and get it over with. After that . . . maybe

Rachel invites us downstairs and we order Chinese food and pass out in front of the TV. I am sure Lytle and Cigar would be on board with that plan. It's been a long, strange trip. We're kind of tired—

"O-o-o-o-scar?" Rachel suddenly says (asks?) with a distinct *oops, I did it again* feel to it.

Only then do I notice her eyebrows are scrunched up. Like a lightning bug got smeared across her forehead (on her birthday). She's waving her stump in the air. No doubt shooting somebody "the finger" with a nonexistent hand. She seems to be staring right through us; scared, angry or both. Cigar now barks it up a notch as Lytle and I turn.

She says my name again, elongated: "O-o-o-o . . . scar."

Then . . . fucking Colonel Sanders . . . Nostril Man, in the flesh, appears from nowhere.

ROCK 'EM SOCK 'EM ROBOTS

OMG. I can't believe this setup . . . Fucking Teeter and Acox two-point-oh. As he, himself, launches fiendishly from behind the rooftop elevator room. Right at us. A cartoon version of a Fed: Suit and tie with aviator shades. Highly polished black non-shoes. Angle-eyed and crazy as a shit-house rat . . . Brandishing a long dog-catcher pole with a noose at the end.

Toe to toe. Gas trapped in a skirt. Something's got to give.

I whirl around. "Rachel? What the fuck?"

"Oscar," she says for the third time. The way she used to say it when we were kids. "All he wants is the dog."

Lytle cries: "Du-ude!"

"That thing is government property, son." Nostril Man is jockeying left and right, noose poised.

Cigar, growling savagely, jumps in front. As something grabs me from behind, I instinctively whirl around, expecting someone to be there, but no one . . . Reaching back defensively, I feel an invisible hairy chest then slide into an even hairier armpit. Ooh, ooh, Dude.

"Oh no, I touched his junk," I hear Lytle lament.

Nostril Man continues his approach, centering his noose while saying: "How long have you kept the animal? Have you ever seen it molt?" Bobbing left, weaving right. "Have you seen the creature? Where did the creature go?" It's like a thousand-mile-an-hour blur.

Mr. Cigar is furiously leading the charge while both Lytle and I are being pushed from behind by a seemingly invisible force. Our eyes meet, and we realize these guys have the IBC video net technology.

Lytle looks absolutely disgusted and confused . . . being pulled/pushed backward by an invisible force . . . grasping a hot dog–shaped object in his right hand while Rachel is repeating, "Oscar, it's the dog; it's the dog!" I scramble beyond grasp . . . vaguely making out the silhouette of a naked invisible man . . . Kind of easy to spot with Mr. Cigar biting at his feet and Lytle's slow-motion death grip on somebody's invisible fireplace tools. I'm almost laughing and rolling right then, standing up at forty-five degrees to Nostril Man, the dogcatcher's pole and the edge of the roof. He's really kind of scary face-to-face. Especially when he's thrusting a noose on a stick and jabbing rapidly . . . first at me and then at Mr. Cigar, who is like a pie-slice serving of a hurricane, attacking everything in front of him but me, Lytle and the airplane overhead. Zero to mayhem in three and a half seconds. Love that guy! Actually, both of 'em.

THE DEAF SCHOOL

For some reason, while this is exploding I can clearly hear my sister rising above the action. "They have this weird machine, Oscar . . ." Obviously, she's referring to the video net technology . . . Nostril Man probably gave her a light show earlier. Nonetheless, I swear, as my sister talks, everybody pauses and has a collective *huh?* moment . . . including Lytle and the invisible man, who are basically in midair falling backward together.

Everything is in slow motion. Nostril Man zeroes in on Mr. Cigar's back legs.

Almost diving to my left and grabbing the end of the dog-catcher's stick with both hands, I plant my feet firmly and pull back, leaning as hard as I can. Nostril Man, standing two or three feet from the edge of the roof, arms outstretched, makes one giant pull of the pole. I hear Lytle say, "Dude!" Cigar barks twice. I am definitely no match for Colonel What's-His-Name as the stick immediately comes out of my hands . . . snaring my left wrist in the process.

OH TWENTY-FOUR HUNDRED!

I get knocked from behind. For a quarter of a breath, I have a tiny bit of leverage. I dig in with my everything, then—*bam*—basically fly toward Nostril Man, who has now rebounded slightly. I impact him high- to midchest. He stumbles slightly. We hit the edge of the roof—which is granite block and a little shorter than my hips. Both of us fall forward/backward and tumble. My feet go to the sky as I see the traffic fourteen stories below—actually, thirteen stories, because this is one of those buildings that doesn't admit to having a thirteenth floor. Apparently bad luck.

—SNAP—

I'm eight years old, lying in bed. Dad is reading to me. I hear his voice like a familiar bell. "'E'll be squattin' on the coals givin' drink to poor damn souls, and I'll get a swig in hell from . . ." Staring up at the ceiling trying to visualize the words, I don't see my father's face, but I can feel him. It feels so safe.

—*CRACK*—

Rolling over into the void, I'm looking up at the sky with upside-down Lytle and Mr. Cigar peering over the edge. Panic in Lytle's voice: "Oscar, n-o-o-o!" Their faces are lit golden by the advancing sun. It's happy hour, and everything is highly detailed, crystal clear, with a blue, blue sky.

—*CRACKLE*—

Tami Ross, the little girl down the block, drags me into the evergreen bushes to show me how little girls wee-wee. A small price to pay for seeing how little boys do the same.

—*EARS RING*—

Totally out of body. I can see my own face close-up, mouth open, frozen as if in surprise. I'm in seventh grade, walking away from the baseball field after quitting the team in the middle of practice, all my teammates pointing at me, chanting, "Pus-sy, pus-sy, pus-sy." As I'm wordlessly leaving the diamond, our coach calls me a faggot, and I've never felt so confidently victorious in my whole fucking life. Ringing now is an oddly static tone. I can still see my face, but it's getting farther and farther away. I feel sorry for that guy. Finally, he disappears into the nothing. BLACK.

NOTHING SADDER THAN A SLOW AMBULANCE

It was raining cats and dogs near Mount Pleasant, Texas—about ninety miles inside the border, just shy of Sulphur Springs. Lytle Falstaff Taylor and a jumpy Mr. Cigar are westbound on Interstate 30. Exhausted, forlorn and miserable, on an endless Monday afternoon.

The storm was so intense they couldn't see their own windshield wipers and had to take refuge under a random farm-road overpass. Free of the rain. In fairly safe vehicular position.

Mr. Cigar is outside the truck barking nervously, and Lytle, standing beside him, crying his eyes out.

This day was easily the worst of young Lytle Taylor's life.

He might see worse. But this was definitely the topper so far. His best friend, Oscar, had died three days before, and it had only gotten sadder since. Who knows? Lytle mused. It may be even more horrible tomorrow.

To Lytle, Oscar's fall—push?—from the SoHo rooftop seemed like five minutes ago. People screaming. People running. Ambulances and a whole bunch of cops. A bizarre disagreement over dog ownership had resulted in unspeakable tragedy. Two people were lost. Lytle didn't know the other guy. Euro-dude left before the police arrived, Rachel said she didn't see "the accident" and Invisible Man just faded into the nothing.

After the authorities left and ambulances slowly pulled away, Lytle sat with Rachel for an hour or two. She was catatonic. He was much the same. Staring in disbelief while petting a magical dog. Near midnight, he found himself downstairs, walking toward the truck with Mr. Cigar. A lame attempt to escape.

They made their way out of the city. Back to Texas, where the music most certainly would play . . . for the both of them.

Lytle drove until he was exhausted, then another hundred miles, passing out for a few minutes—cycle and repeat. Driving on. Halfway between Nashville and Memphis, he finally gave up. Following a Waffle House–sedative breakfast, he collapsed at a rest stop. Dreaming of nothing. Guarded by Mr. Cigar. Following the much-needed sleep, they were then back on the interstate, heading into an ominous horizon of gray-green thunderclouds. Eventually, they found themselves under the overpass, waiting for a break in the storm . . . about three hours from home.

Cigar had been nervous, pacing—back and forth, left and right—ever since Texarkana. After the pair were sidelined by the deluge, he leapt from the truck, ran to a damp patch of sand then began barking loudly while pawing intently at the dirt. Lytle remained inside the truck, unblinking and fragile, seeing nothing other than Oscar's body, lying thirteen stories below.

Something about Mr. Cigar's demeanor, however, prompted Lytle to snap out of it and see what the hubbub was all about.

Lytle got out of the truck and to his amazement, right below Cigar's barking muzzle, the letters O-S-C-A-R were clearly scratched into the pliable sand.

"Oh, ma-a-an," Lytle mournfully elongated.

Then he crumbled. Seeing the name pawed into the earth, he assumed two things: this was a trick Oscar had taught his four-legged compatriot, and, of course, Mr. Cigar truly missed their mutual friend.

"I love you, buddy-y-y-y," Lytle added, longer and louder, echoing through the concrete shelter. Sorrow had finally hit its mark. Big tears now. Big enough to drain the Texas sky. The clouds above the overpass cracked as bright sunlight mercifully sang through the waning storm. The tears kept rolling down the young man's cheeks and the devil was beating his wife.

His phone rang.

It was Carla Marks.

Lytle hesitated . . . then answered, "Carla?"

"Hey, sweetheart. How are you doing?"

"I'm okay," a sobbing Lytle replied.

"Aww, honey, things aren't as bad as you think they are. You should come by IBC before you go home, sweetie. I talked to your mom, and she's fine with it. She's okay for as long as it takes. We actually have a LoJack device on the video net unit and know where you are. Just be careful. I love you. Try not to be sad. It's weird, I know. Listen to some Nirvana or Patsy Cline, something Oscar would like. Just no opera . . . I'll see you in a couple of hours?"

"Okay, Carla."

"I promise you it's going to be all right," soothed Carla. "Just come by IBC. How's Mr. Cigar, by the way? Is he behaving oddly?"

Lytle paused. "Well, actually . . . it was raining so hard we stopped under an overpass, and Cigar got out and scratched Oscar's name in the dirt. It's crazy; I know it must have been some trick Oscar taught him . . . but it seemed so real, like he was doing it himself."

"That's interesting, Lytle," Carla murmured. "Mr. Cigar is quite a dog . . . I'm looking at the weather near you, and it's clearing up. Take your time and I'll see you in a bit."

Lytle, strangely relieved, got back on the road with Patsy Cline, Cigar and his last twenty dollars for gas.

In no time Lytle arrived at the Itty Bitty Corporation, parked near the front door and walked inside with the video unit and Mr. Cigar in tow.

A waiting Carla abruptly barked like a dog at Mr. Cigar. Then she gave Lytle a big hug and said, "Welcome, sweetheart."

Mr. Cigar barked back.

Lytle was confused, to say the least.

Carla gestured—the palms-out, fingers-up, *wait a second, it'll be cool* deal—and added, "Follow me upstairs. You're gonna freak out."

Dumbfounded, Lytle shadowed her down the hall and into a stairwell. Every now and then, Carla barked, apparently into the ether. Again, Mr. Cigar barked back. Carla smiled. When they reached the top, Carla opened the door onto the roof—kind of like the roof in SoHo, but no feds or family members.

"Mr. Cigar has had quite a wild life, Lytle," Carla began. "Well . . . I'll just cut to the chase. The best way to describe it is . . . Oscar is now Mr. Cigar."

Lytle blinked at her. "What?"

Cig barked, and Carla barked back.

"Lytle," she said, "I don't know if Oscar ever told you, but I've been able to talk to animals since I was a child."

"Yeah, I know," Lytle replied nervously, his eyes darting between Carla and his best friend's beloved pet. "Oscar told me about it, but I thought that it was more of a symbolic *I know nature* kind of thing . . ."

"No, Lytle. I can actually talk to animals. Insects too."

"Jesus, Carla, what do bugs say?" Lytle heard himself ask.

"More than you would think," she answered. "Much more. Not so much individually. But as a group, there is a wealth of information. Anyway . . ."

"So my best friend is a dog now? What about girls?"

"Lytle," Carla scolded mildly.

Mr. Cigar growled.

Carla, clearly prepared, motioned toward a shallow box of sand placed here for the occasion.

"Lytle . . . Ask Oscar or Mr. Cigar any question you want," she said. "Something only Oscar would know. At least something a dog wouldn't know. And keep it to a two- or three-word answer. You can't write a book in this sandbox."

Lytle, brow furrowed, bent down and extended a hand to the dog. In a condescending tone, he said, "Okay, buddy . . . shake."

"Lytle!" Carla chided, this time more sternly.

Cigar remained motionless, growling.

"I'm sorry," Lytle offered in frustration. He straightened, his throat tightening. "It's just that it's really kind of hard to take seriously. My best friend died—like last night."

"I know but not really," Carla interrupted. Her face softened. "Oh, honey. Just ask Oscar a question."

Accessing memory, eyeballs skyward, Lytle paused for a two-count then doubtfully said, "Okay, dog, dude, whatever . . . What's my middle name?"

Mr. Cigar flexed to the sandbox and scratched out the letters *D-U-M-B-A-S-S*. He stared defiantly back at Lytle.

Carla chuckled. "Lytle, I'm afraid you walked into that one."

Lytle shook his head. He wasn't convinced. Maybe he didn't want to be convinced. "Yeah, but that could still be a—"

Before he could finish, before the word "trick" came out, Cigar had scratched *F-A-L-S-T-A-F-F* in the remaining space.

"Holy shit, buddy. Is that really you?"

Cigar wagged his tail madly and ran at Lytle. Jumping into his arms, *not* licking his face.

"Holy shit," Lytle repeated, a true believer now. Astonishment and joy melted away any lingering sorrow. He turned to Carla. "But . . . how?"

She beamed. "I told you Cigar had an interesting life, Lytle. I'm sure that, eventually, all will be revealed, and I'm also sure that we're *all* going to have an interesting life . . . together. Now come over here and check this out."

Carla walked to a ten-foot-square piece of what looked like Astroturf laid out on the Itty Bitty rooftop. She asked for all to have a seat in the middle—Carla and Lytle crosslegged, Oscar the dog between them. The surface was soft and cushiony.

"Here's the freaky part," Carla said. "I call it the MC-5." She snapped her fingers.

At the sharp noise, the entire rug thing rose five feet into the air—somehow keeping all on board, in perfect balance, gliding toward the edge of the building.

Lytle, now reeling from this psychedelic information overload, obscenely crescendoed a stream of "Holy shit, holy shit, holy shit!"

"Yep . . . the Magic Carpet Five!" Carla announced proudly. She shrugged. "The first four versions were duds."

"How the fuck, Carla?" Lytle asked, peering over the edge. The ground far below.

"Good question, Lytle. It's kind of complicated, but it began with a wonderful conversation I had with a group of hummingbirds . . ."

Lytle sat in silent wonder, beaming incredulously as they floated forward into a gorgeous magenta-orange Texas sky, known in this neck of the woods as a "cowboy sunset"—a reference that surprisingly had nothing to do with football, cheerleaders or oil. Slowly returning to a state of realization, gazing wide-eyed to the west, Lytle spoke in a serious monotone. "Guys? We're gonna rule the fucking world."

Oscar/Cigar barked for several seconds. Carla smiled then barked in response. Oscar began to wag his tail.

"What did he say?" Lytle whispered.

"He said, 'Don't think "world," Lytle. Think "universe"!'"

"And what did you say back?"

"I said, 'Don't be silly, guys. We're not going to *rule* the universe. We're going to fix it.'"

Lytle Falstaff Taylor laughed. He closed his eyes and let the warm Texas wind rush over his face. "Wow, Carla, where do we begin with that one?"

"At the end, Lytle," she said. "Right at the end."

ACKNOWLEDGMENTS

Special thanks to mother and daddy-o and the rest of the crew on Buxhill Drive for providing a place of comfort that will forever be there in times of need . . .

Thanks to Daniel E, my editor, for providing literary, monetary, and psychiatric assistance during the production of *Me & Mr. Cigar* . . . and to the entire Soho Press crew—especially Publisher Bronwen, Publicist Paul, Design Genius Janine, Sharp-Eyed Rachel, and Kindred Spirit Mark—and on top of that, everyone on the Children's Sales Force at Penguin Random House.

Thanks to these authors and likeminded souls: Jeff Zentner, Garth Stein, Geoff Herbach, and Blake Nelson.

Special thanks as well to the Richardson Independent School District . . . I owe you at least $5,000.

Special no-thanks to Jerry Kramer, who was clearly offsides in the waning moments of the ice-bowl goal-line stand.

Thanks also to my bandmates, the Butthole Surfers, and to Dandy Don Meredith (the inventor of the bomb) and Bob Hayes #22 (the fastest man on earth).